Onwards & Upwards

Onwards & Upwards

by

Eugenie Summerfield

G&G

Copyright © Eugenie Summerfield 2010
First published in 2010 by Greenman & Greenman
11 Woodgate Close
Barnwood, Glos, GL4 3TN

www.amolibros.com

Distributed by Gardners Books
1 Whittle Drive, Eastbourne, East Sussex, BN23 6QH
Tel: +44(0)1323 521555 | Fax: +44(0)1323 521666

All the characters in this book are fictitious and any resemblance to
actual people, living or dead, is purely imaginary.

British Library Cataloguing in Publication Data
A catalogue record for this book is available from the British Library

ISBN 978-0-9565531-0-2

Typeset by Amolibros, Milverton, Somerset
This book production has been managed by Amolibros
Printed and bound by T J International Ltd, Padstow, Cornwall, UK

About the Author

Many authors take up writing for children after a successful career in adult fiction. With *Onwards & Upwards* Eugenie Summerfield has made the switch the other way round. She is already known to a wide audience through TV, radio and books for children, her 'Wonderful Wriggly Worm' stories on BBC programmes having attracted listeners young and old over many years. Now in her 'golden age' Eugenie has turned her attention to adult readers with her first novel *Onwards & Upwards*; a 'fun read' with its quirky and original tone, which will appeal to a broad readership.

Eugenie Summerfield has three grown-up children and now lives in Gloucestershire where, when she isn't writing, she spends as much time as possible in her small 'secret garden', which provides much of her inspiration.

For Steven,
James, Caroline and Angela

"The theme explores the affinity between tragedy and farce, and it is enhanced by an entertaining style. I found it hard to put down."

Lord Archer of Sandwell

"*Onwards and Upwards* is a cheesy tale in the most flavoursome sense of the word. The delightful lightness of its crust gives way to a wickedly pungent humour at its core."

Caroline Sanderson, The Bookseller

"It is a real page-turner and I found it witty, compelling and very amusing. The opening sentences draw one in immediately. I chuckled a lot – especially at the *Times* 'Matches Hatches and Dispatches' section: never heard that one before!"

David Bell, radio and television producer

"A bizarre death is the backdrop to Eugenie Summerfield's first excursion into adult fiction. As an already successful children's writer, she has now moved into a more complex world peopled by a fascinating collection of believable characters all of whom have a link with the unusual death. It's a tale of misunderstandings and mistaken identities which is both tragic and comic. *Onwards and Upwards* is an effortless read flowing easily from one scene and character to another...ideal mental relaxation for bedtimes or holidays."

John Lovell

What will survive of us is love'
(from *Whitsun Weddings* by Philip Larkin)

Prelude

L iz, this is Margot Prettiflower. I hope you remember me..."

"Margot! Is that *really* you? How are you? I thought you were dead."

Oh dear! *Not* the best of beginnings. Maybe I shouldn't have rung her. But Liz Marley was after all still my agent, wasn't she?

"No-o Liz," I faltered, " that wasn't me. It was..."

I wasn't sure how to go on. It was still very difficult to talk to anyone, least of all to Liz Marley, about what had actually happened. I'd always felt somewhat intimidated by her whenever we'd met in the past. To my mind, she epitomised the highly successful modern woman, in fact everything that I was not. She was always so perfectly groomed in her black Armani suits and flawless make-up. Never a shining hair of her bobbed head out of place. I felt dowdy beside her in my 'country classic' clothes and sensible shoes.

I could only assume she must have been idly scanning through the Births, Marriages and Deaths in *The Times,* and jumped to the wrong conclusion about what had happened to Marcus.

Now I came to think about it, maybe that notice had been just a bit too brief. I really should have given more information, his full name for instance rather than just his initial. And I should have said something about the tragic circumstances of

Marcus's death, shouldn't I? But then, you don't think straight at times like that, do you?

I suppose I was worried about the expense. It's not cheap, you know – dying, these days. You see, I'd never had much to do with the handling of our financial affairs throughout our marriage. Marcus took care of all that.

All the same, that notice should have been a bit more specific, even if it had cost me a bit more. It should have read "Prettiflower, Marcus, beloved husband of Margot, died suddenly on January 10th in Saltledale, North Yorkshire, as the result of a tragic accident. Much mourned by all who knew him…"or something to that effect.

Marcus, my darling Marcus…I don't suppose the name meant anything to Liz anyway, but to me – it meant the whole world. A whole lost world.

"Well Margot?"

She sounded cagey. I sensed she was none too pleased by my untimely interruption. I could picture her sitting there, drumming her well manicured nails against the surface of her desk waiting impatiently for me to go on. She was probably wondering why I'd rung her out of the blue. After all, I hadn't been in touch with her for ages, although we had worked very closely at one time. But that tactless opening remark of hers made me wonder if she'd forgotten all about me.

It was my old school friend, Cathy Goodson, who had first introduced me to Liz Marley ages ago. Cathy is a highly successful writer of romantic fiction. You've most likely heard of her or read some of her books. They're always on the bestseller lists. So it was Cathy who insisted I should get in touch with Liz again.

"You've got to think about the future, now duckie, not the past," Cathy had said quite bluntly, just after the cremation. "Move on. Onwards and upwards, that should be your aim now. You've a whole new life ahead of you. And believe me, not having a man in one's life to worry about is wonderfully stimulating, creatively speaking. I should know."

I gathered, from this remark of hers, that Cathy was not at that time 'in a relationship'. But knowing her as well as I did, I guessed that this was merely a temporary state of affairs. She being a serial romantic.

"So get writing again. Do some research first though, since it'll be a whole new territory for you. Why not take a leaf out of my book – not literally, of course."

She'd presented me with a copy of her own latest best-seller *Bed of Roses,* which was not, as you might have imagined a book on gardening. You had only to look at the lurid cover to see that.

It was of course, like all Cathy's other books – a passionate love story. They usually feature irresistibly handsome heroes, endowed with every desirable attribute – physically and materially, who fall hopelessly in love with a plain Jane Eyre type of heroine. Not really my kind of thing. I much prefer the classics. A Jane Austen or a Trollope, at bedtime will invariably soothe me off to sleep after a paragraph or two.

I was still in a state of shock. But then, so many things have happened since Marcus's sudden demise which set me thinking that maybe Cathy was right. Now was the time to think about the future, not dwell upon the past. Marcus never did. That was one of the things which I most admired about him and which had endeared him to me.

Cathy is the kind of person you don't say 'no' to. So that's how it was that I got in touch with Liz Marley again and put through an early morning call to her office. I was hoping she'd be as enthusiastic as I was about my new sense of direction when I'd sketched out a few details. Unless of course she'd changed somewhat since the old days when we had worked closely together.

★★★

The call came straight through to me at 8.35 a.m. Eight-thirty-five, I ask you!

I'm a great believer in making an early start but I hadn't even had time to switch my voice mail on, check my e-mails or snatch a quick cup of coffee. I couldn't imagine what dinosaur would be phoning me at that time of day, instead of e-mailing or faxing. Margot Prettiflower. That's who it was. You could have knocked me down with the Shorter Oxford English Dictionary. *I thought she was dead! In fact I was almost sure I'd seen her name in the 'Dispatches' columns of the 'Matches Hatches and Dispatches' in* The Times *not long ago.*

'Prettiflower…' It's an eye-catching sort of name. There can't be many of them around. Must have been some kind of relative of hers, I suppose.

Obviously, Margot, herself, was still in the land of the living because there she was going on and on about some new thing she'd dreamed up and wanted to send me. Something to do with the Renaissance as far as I could gather. Although I wasn't quite sure because it didn't sound at all like the sort of thing she wrote, as far as I could remember. I was pretty certain historical fact, or fiction, was not her forte.

I didn't want to be unkind to the poor old bat. After all, she had been a good client of Daniel, Robson and Learby back in the old days when her 'Pinkie the Elephant' series were very popular with the kids and even grown-ups as well, though some sour critic in one of the tabloids attributed this to subversive left-wing undertones and Freudian nuances. From what I knew of her, she wasn't like that. And you know what they say, 'to the pure in heart all things are pure'. So it probably said a great deal more about him *than it did about Margot.*

Anyway, things have changed a bit since those days, especially in the market for kids' lit. It's mostly aimed at teenagers now — social

4

'realism', kids in Care Homes or weirdo boarding schools, horror stories, vampires, creatures from Outer Space — that kind of thing. That's what my best clients produce nowadays. It's what kids want and it's what sells and brings in the money. No cuddly cute animals, nothing twee or whimsical, definitely not these days. No, unless the old dear had changed a lot, I was pretty certain Margot wouldn't stand an earthly with whatever it was she was intending to write about now. How was I going to break it to her gently?

I tried desperately to cut her short but she was unstoppable. I think she'd just said, "so this isn't going to be a book for children this time. It will be a very adult novel — lots of steamy sex and all that sort of thing. So of course I'll have to get myself a computer and do quite a bit of research first."

Steamy sex and Margot Prettiflower? It sounded most unlikely for her and I really couldn't figure out the connection between sex and computers, unless of course she was thinking of exploring one of those internet chat-rooms. No, I just couldn't imagine that.

If my memory served me right, she was somewhat prissy, quasi-Victorian almost in her outlook. I couldn't even remember whether she was married or not because she never talked about her private life, which was unusual in the author/agent relationship.

Mind you, my mind was wandering somewhat. I was thinking I ought to put through a call to lover-boy, Alex, on his mobile before he boarded his flight for Frankfurt, and tell him how fantastic he'd been last night. I hadn't had a chance to speak to him before he went this morning. He must have left at some ungodly hour before I was awake, in order to get to the airport. well ahead of time, which was unusual for him. He's very much a last-minute, all-in-a-rush kind of guy.

Must have crept out, so as not to disturb me, without making all those maddening stamping, splashing and tuneless singing noises which he usually does when he's in the shower. And, he'd left everything so tidy, too — cleared all his clutter away, even taken his toothbrush *and his smelly socks! That was very considerate of him. He can be such a poppet sometimes – which got me thinking I'd make a romantic candlelit dinner à deux. His favourite meal. Boeuf Béarnaise, and a sinful chocolate mousse to welcome him back from Frankfurt on Monday evening. He'd be bound to be shattered after his assignment there and in need of some tlc. Something his ghastly wife was incapable of giving him, poor lamb, from what he's told me. She never cooked him a decent meal and she'd even refused to do his laundry because of those smelly socks of his. Why he hadn't dumped her ages ago beats me. Maybe Monday evening would be a good time to broach that subject again with him. It was high time our relationship was put onto a firmer footing.*

Meanwhile, I managed to drag my thoughts back to Margot. At last I was able to put my spoke in. She'd just said, "…and that's what people want these days, isn't it?" I don't know what she was referring to.

My mind was still on sexy, adorable Alex, so I rashly agreed wholeheartedly. Then I said,

"Margot, darling, I've got to go off to a meeting in a minute so why don't you send me a synopsis of your new novel and the first three chapters, then we can take it on from there?"

As I replaced the receiver, I thought to myself that I'd most likely never hear from her again. How wrong can you be?

2

I expect you're wondering about the events which preceded my decision to start writing again. So I should point out right away that it was not until very much later that I, myself, found out what had really happened to Marcus and the events surrounding his 'accident'. There were, of course, one or two gaps where I've had to use my imagination. But so that you'll understand the tragedy in its entirety, let me tell you, clearly and sincerely, in my own words the whole story right from the very beginning.

★★★

It really shouldn't have happened. What a way to start the New Year – or rather in Marcus's case, not start it. It was so unexpected and so bizarre the way Marcus met his tragic death that day.

I mean, you may well have heard of Aeschylus, that is if you are a lover of Greek tragic drama. In which case you will know that Aeschylus's life was unfortunately cut short when a tortoise was dropped on his bald head by an eagle flying overhead, in the mistaken belief, so it was said, that Aeschylus's bald head was a suitable stone for breaking tortoise shells. And you may have read about that sort of thing in fiction. There was that story, by Graham Green I think it was, about the pig on a balcony in Italy, but in real life…well, it rarely happens – not to my knowledge anyway. And for anyone reading this now, I hope you will take due note of what happened to Marcus and be extra careful when you're walking through narrow passageways in an area where there are ancient buildings with overhanging balconies, or anywhere else for that matter, so that it will never happen again. You never know what might be *Up There* waiting to descend upon you out of the blue.

If only I'd remembered to put his usual Danish Blue sandwiches and a Cox's orange pippin into Marcus's brief-case that morning, he might still be alive today. But then, life is full of 'if onlys', isn't it?

How different our lives would be *if only* we could live them backwards. Starting off with all the knowledge of what we should, or should not, have done throughout our lives! All the wrongs we'd committed in the rawness of youth, we could put right, using the after-knowledge we'd acquired as mature individuals. We'd be *so* confident. None of the agonising uncertainties of youth to trouble us, as to whether our acne would ever go away, or whether we would ever recover from the heart-break of broken romances when we thought we would never love, or be loved by anyone again. Not only that, we'd be so much more loveable if we could end our days as adorable cuddly babies, soft skinned and bright-eyed, rather than the wrinkly, crotchety old crones we become, '*sans teeth, sans eyes, sans taste, sans everything*'. Ah well, that's just not possible even in this age of scientific and technological advancement, so we have to live with our mistakes and the consequences of them.

The irony of it was that Marcus loved cheese and, for reasons I'll explain later, he was in the process of becoming quite an authority on every aspect of the origins and manufacture of all kinds of cheese. You might almost say he was passionate about it. So to be killed by one…at such a time, in such a place…in a small Yorkshire town where such happenings had never been known before. Well, that was just too much.

It was one of those enormous solid round cheeses which weigh goodness knows how many kilos. The sort they pitch down a hill in Gloucestershire in an annual cheese rolling contest. I believe it dates back to some ancient fertility rites in Spring. People can get quite badly injured when this happens – the cheese rolling, I mean – not the fertility rites; much to the annoyance of the hard-pressed members of staff at the A&E Department of the local hospital.

3

Daft present to send to a firm of lawyers that cheese was, if you ask me, even if it was from the most grateful of clients. No wonder no one at Smethers and Lybrand knew what to do with it. They even claimed not to know who exactly had sent it to them.

It was pathetic the way that cheese had apparently been hanging around in its rather tatty and torn 'Happy Christmas' wrapping in their tiny office kitchen for days, if not weeks. Until that is someone went and complained loudly about the smell to Charles Hardy, the senior partner.

Charles, up to that point in time, had been happily unaware of the cheese. The pungent aroma had not bothered him. His office, being at the rear of the building, was fortunately not in close proximity to the office kitchen and, as it so happened, he did not have a particularly finely tuned sense of smell.

Well before the Christmas Office Party season had begun, staff members with sensitive noses had already remarked several times on the unpleasant aroma which had even permeated their tea and coffee, or so they said. But, it wasn't until the office reopened after the New Year Bank holiday that the smell had become so pervasive that even Charles Hardy was forced to take notice and really got things moving in every sense of the word.

Charles was not in the best of moods that morning. He and his wife, Sandra, had been to a dinner party the night before and had returned home very late. The food and the wines had been excellent, especially the delicious selection of cheeses, of which Charles had partaken rather freely, to round off the meal. Charles, never any good at dinner party small talk, was then anxious to get home to bed, in preparation for the pressing demands of work to be done the following day in the office.

Sandra, too, was eager to get to bed for other reasons. Just one glass of good red wine invariably had a surprisingly aphrodisiac effect on her. She had dressed with great care that evening. She was wearing her latest designer green silk dress, matching jade necklace and ear-rings which enhanced the burnished copper sheen of her hair. She was well aware that she was the focus of admiration from the male guests and of envy from the other women at the dinner table. Not unreasonably, she was hoping that, after what for her had been a most enjoyable evening, a night of passion with Charles would surely follow. Unfortunately, however, and much to her disappointment, Charles did not rise to her expectations.

It was hardly surprising in the circumstances therefore that the day had started badly. Sandra was in a most resentful mood. Charles, too, was not in the best of tempers. He had not slept well, for which he blamed the cheese. And, over breakfast that morning, he not only remarked several times to Sandra that his stomach was still feeling somewhat queasy after last night but that he also thought he 'might be going down with something nasty'.

He was at a loss to understand why these remarks were not greeted at all sympathetically by Sandra, who merely glared at him with silent resentment over the breakfast table. He couldn't imagine what was niggling her. Perhaps the previous evening meal had disagreed with her too. Or perhaps for her it was that time of the month, which so often made women unpredictably moody, he surmised. Anyway, women were used to that sort of thing, weren't they? Whereas men, on those rare occasions when their lower regions were afflicted, needed to be shown sympathy and understanding by their women-folk. Well, it was apparent that no such concern was forthcoming from Sandra on this particular morning, he thought somewhat bitterly. She'd not even given him a good morning kiss and there she was hardly saying a word to him but snapping at the children.

The children, Veronica, Fiona and Nicola were playing up in the way children do, when surfeited with toys and games, in the post-Christmas days of anti-climax. To make matters worse, Monique, their latest nanny, who usually kept them in order at this time of day, had not come down to join them for breakfast that morning.

"She's got a poorly tummy," volunteered Vanessa, his eldest daughter.

"A poorly tummy," echoed Fiona, the second Hardy offspring.

"Is she having a baby?" asked Nicola, the youngest, hopefully.

It had not gone unnoticed in the Hardy household that Nicola had been in a constant sulk ever since Christmas Day. Her faith in Father Christmas had been severely shaken this year. Although she no longer really believed in him, she had written him several letters detailing her specific wishes so that the message would be clearly understood and passed on to her wealthy maternal grandparent in good time for all the necessary arrangements to be made for the delivery of her present for Christmas.

To Nicola's bitter disappointment, instead of the pony she had specifically requested, a copy of *Black Beauty* had arrived for her. And, even if it was a valuable first edition, signed by the author, as her mother was anxious to point out, it was, in Nicola's opinion, downright mean on the part of her grandfather.

However, now a sudden smile replaced the scowl on her face. She brightened at the idea of a new baby in the New Year as a suitable substitute. She sighed dreamily.

" Wouldn't it be lovely if Monique does have a baby?"

"I damn well hope not!" muttered Charles under his breath.

"Well then, if she doesn't, couldn't *we* have a baby instead?"

A quick glance at Sandra was enough to convince Charles that a somewhat awkward conversation was likely to develop around the breakfast table at any moment. He'd leave her to deal with Nicola's unanswered question. She was so much better at that sort of thing. No need for him to get involved.

Hurriedly abandoning his half-consumed coffee, he decided to make a quick exit for his study, to gather up his papers and brief case, and depart as soon as possible for the busy day ahead of him at the office. He had enough worries in his working life without additional complications on the domestic front.

And, to crown it all, when he was about to set off for the office rather later than he had intended that morning, the BMW refused to start.

"Women!" he fumed. It was all Sandra's fault that the damn car wouldn't start. She'd insisted on driving the car home after the party last night since, as she smugly pointed out – *she* had kept well within the legal limit for alcohol should they be stopped and breathalysed by some over-zealous copper.

"And you know what they can be like when they're dealing with lawyers, don't you, darling?" she'd reminded him.

He hated it when Sandra drove his car. She was hopeless at parking, even when she was driving her own little Mini. So she had not even attempted to navigate his car into the garage and had left it standing at a very awkward angle out on the drive all night in Arctic conditions, which added further to Charles's irritation.

He was late for his first appointment when he finally reached the office and there on his desk, was yet another of those crazy anonymous letters addressed to Mr. Smethers and/or Mr. Lybrand.

"Dear Sirs," it said, "What goes on in your office has got to stop or steps will be taken to put an end to the hanky panky. Yours truly, A well wisher."

He supposed the letter had been fabricated by some disgruntled client. Clearly someone with a deranged mind.

Didn't the idiot who was writing these letters realise that both these venerable gentlemen had been dead, for quite some time? Or as good as, in the case of old Matthew Lybrand junior, who in his last few years with the firm had spent most of his time dozing at his desk over the cryptic crossword in *The Times*, until the other partners had persuaded him it was high time for him to retire to the comfort of his imposing Edwardian mock-Tudor mansion deep in the heart of the North Yorkshire Country Parkland. So no one bearing these names existed at the firm now.

Although, there was a rumour, probably started by some silly typist who was scared of big black spiders, that the ghost of old Toby Smethers still haunted the damp dark basement offices, where ancient Wills were kept. Charles supposed that there might be the odd rat or two down there, but certainly no ghosts of any description.

Charles sighed in exasperation and, crumpling the letter into a ball, tossed it straight into the waste-paper basket. Nevertheless, this added irritation plunged his already black mood further into darkness. So, when he was informed by Amy, one of the senior secretaries, of the smelly cheese problem, his immediate response was to march straight into the office kitchen, fling open the window, hurl the offending object out onto the somewhat rusty wrought-iron ice-encrusted balcony and slam the window shut, firmly announcing as he did so, "And that takes care of that!"

On his return to his own office, Charles felt much better for this decisive action. So much so that he scribbled himself a memo to buy Sandra a bunch of flowers from Floribunda, the florists across the street on his way home that evening. And he would perhaps look into the off-license for a bottle of that wine he and she had enjoyed so much at last night's dinner party. That should help to cheer the old girl up. He thought she had still been somewhat down in the mouth when he left home that morning No parting kiss. Not even a peck on the cheek. Goodness knows why! Apart that is from that usual feminine inconvenience, he supposed.

Strange creatures – women. He'd never really quite understood what went on in their minds. All the same, he adored her and thought she was looking quite good for her age at yesterday's party. That clinging green thing she was wearing really showed off her figure and complimented her gorgeous red hair. He had noticed somewhat smugly that the other male guests at the dinner party thought so too. He was a very lucky man to have such a stunner as his wife, he told himself. Yes, he'd certainly spoil her a bit when he got home tonight.

Meanwhile, those few members of staff of Messrs. Smethers and Lybrand who were around at the time, applauded Charles' action, thinking they could now breathe freely again. But nothing could be further from the truth. That was not the end of the matter…oh no…it was just the beginning.

4

Fate had decreed that on that murky afternoon in early January Marcus, having discovered the lunch-less state of his briefcase and prompted no doubt by pangs of hunger, was taking a short-cut through Friargate Passage on his way to the nearest coffee bar before returning to the Reference Library, where judging from the sheaf of most meticulous notes in his brief case when it was examined later, he had had a very rewarding morning researching into his favourite subject, which curiously enough, as I mentioned earlier and will explain more fully later, was all to do with cheese.

So, it was most unfortunate that with his mind, no doubt, focused on other matters, he was directly below that murderous object as it came crashing down upon him. Poor dear Marcus, I would like to think that his last conscious thoughts were happy ones.

How much damage the cheese itself suffered remains something of a mystery, since after hearing what had happened to Marcus, nobody was prepared to admit to having had anything to do with it and indeed wished to deny any knowledge whatsoever of it, especially the personnel of Messrs Smethers and Lybrand, who foresaw all kinds of litigious consequences arising.

In case you should be wondering about the apple and the Danish Blue sandwiches (it was wholegrain bread, by the way) and thinking what kind of a wife would be treating her beloved husband's stomach in such a way, I'd better explain about Marcus and me. We had now reached the age when we were paddling about in the quiet waters of the male retirement era, after having weathered more or less successfully the choppy seas of the male menopausal years. I say *male* retirement era quite deliberately because there is no such thing as retirement for us females with long-standing male partners. Of course, things may be different for you younger readers, or if you are in an all-female relationship but I don't really know about that.

Being of the pre-women's liberation generation, and having been brought up in an all female household by two very strict and strait-laced women – my mother and my grandmother, in the immediate post WWII era, I had been conditioned into believing that the woman's role was in the home. And so, right from the very start of my marriage to Marcus, faithfully adhering the teachings of my mother and grandmother, I strove to achieve domestic perfection. I also slavishly followed the edicts of the women's magazines of that era and the advertisements on TV – commercial television having newly entered our lives around that time.

Apart from those mornings when we weren't speaking to one another, Marcus was always sent off to work with a dutiful kiss, after his man-sized high cholesterol breakfasts of bacon, sausage, mushrooms and egg. That was the best possible start for the day at that time. The Egg Marketing Board exhorted us to "Go to work on an egg". Not just any old egg, but ones stamped with the British lion showing they were British through and through. So, I really felt it was my patriotic duty to make sure that Marcus should have the best of British start to his working day. Because, although he never said so openly, I sensed it was important for Marcus to feel 'more British than the British' in this, his adopted country.

After his departure to the office, I used to set about making the house immaculate and always had his dinner on the table when he returned in the early evening from his harrowing working day. Marcus never talked to me much about his work, which was 'in Sales' in the import and export business. I assumed it must be very wearing and deadly dull, judging by the business associates and their wives I met through occasional enforced social contact, when I was expected to hostess dinner parties for them.

Fortunately, in those early days, I really enjoyed cooking, using family recipes handed down by my grandmother, trying out new recipes, painstakingly clipped out of glossy magazine like *Good Housekeeping* and jotting down cookery hints from TV programmes.

Like many other raw young housewives eager to please their dinner guests in the early 1960s, I slavishly followed the instructions of Fanny Cradock, as she, in glamorous make-up, jewellery and ball-gown, demonstrated to us on TV with the aid of her partner, Johnny, how ridiculously simple it was to make all manner of culinary works of art for our sophisticated dinner parties. Delicacies such as canapés, prawn cocktails, Maypole chicken and exotic green cheese ice-cream. I tried them all. It may have been simple for Fanny and Johnny but it actually took me hours and hours attempting to replicate her fleet of meringue swans, floating on an icing sugar 'lake' as a sensational centre-piece for one of our less successful dinner parties Unfortunately, my 'swans' were a *Titanic* disaster.

All that time and effort was more often than not unrewarding for me, even if these gourmet meals did, on the whole, help to enhance the sale of imports and exports for Marcus. Those being the early days of 'never having had it so good' as we were told by a prominent politician of the day, conversation among guests round the dinner table nearly always took the form of one-man-upmanship. The men competing against one another with detailed descriptions of recently acquired cars, sailing boats, time-share properties, that sort of thing. The women enthusing about their offsprings' latest outstanding academic and/or athletic achievements in their cripplingly expensive private or public schools, or complaining about the outrageous exploits of their latest au pairs, which rather cut me out of the conversation with the business associate wives. I couldn't contribute any amusing little family anecdotes because of Marcus and my failure in becoming parents.

This never seemed to unsettle Marcus, solicitous host as always, discretely in the background making sure their wine glasses were always topped up, so that the constant flow of chit-chat never dried up. *They* were all having an enjoyable evening, which was all that mattered as far as he was concerned. But it left me after the last guest had gone, feeling somehow inadequate and unfulfilled, and quite often, at the end of the day, desperately tearful.

Although, I suppose I was lucky in a way in that eventually I discovered a creative outlet, apart from domestic duties. You see, I was able eventually to find fulfilment in other ways, after Marcus and I had had several exhaustive and unsuccessful attempts to produce a baby. What a harrowing time that was. All that business with thermometers and calendar dates made love-making more of a chore than a spontaneous pleasure.

We had tried everything, well, practically everything. Although, I had drawn the line at one of Cathy's more fanciful suggestions. I have mentioned her before, haven't I? Cathy Goodson and I had been friends ever since our school days. I admired her for her tremendous imagination. It was her suggestion that Marcus and I should go to Paris one Spring, so that I could spend a night stretched out upon the tomb of a certain Victor Noir, whose bronze bulging member was said to be a sure cure for infertility. I really couldn't imagine how that would work.

We had even completely exhausted ourselves and acquired a strong dislike for fish for a while, as a result of having read somewhere of high birth rates among Catholics nine months after Lent. It might work for Catholics but it certainly didn't work for us. So it was something of a relief to give up trying. We hoped that by allowing Nature to take its course we just might be blessed with a child but we never were.

It was really thanks to another suggestion of Cathy's that I turned my disappointment into creation of another kind. I began writing stories for all the children I could never have. Dear Cathy, on one of her flying visit to us, it was she, who finding me plunged yet again into utter misery by my inability to conceive, reminded me that I had always been something of a story-teller in our school days. She could even remember some of the tales I had once told and which I had completely forgotten.

She, in those far-off school days, being spindly legged and short-sighted, was never very good at competitive sports and we both disliked the playground battles at break-times. Cathy and I would huddle by the radiator in a corner of the junior girls' cloakroom, where she and I would regale one another with our latest works of fiction, until we were turfed out for fresh air and exercise by some power-mad prefect.

My stories were usually about the adventures of cuddly, furry animals – rabbits, mice, squirrels – that sort of thing, whereas Cathy's imagination roamed much wider into tales of romantic love, all with happy-ever-after endings. So it was hardly surprising that in adult life she became a prolific and highly successful writer of romantic fiction.

Not that either of us knew anything much about *making love,* as it was called in those days. It wasn't referred to as *sex* then. As far as we were concerned the word 'sex' meant being either male or female. Coming to terms with puberty for Cathy and me brought the shock of discovering certain surprisingly unwelcome facts relating to our female anatomy.

Burgeoning breasts were OK. Much admired film stars of that era were role models for the fully grown version of those. We could hardly wait to introduce our tiny swelling pink mounds into our first brassieres. But it was that other *thing* which Cathy and I commiserated over in private – being stuck from now on with all that messy monthly inconvenience.

How typical of a vengeful Old Testament God to foist *that* on Eve rather than on Adam, along with the burden of pregnancy and then giving birth! After all, it was from Adam's body that God had brought forth Eve in the first place, wasn't it? What was wrong with that method of reproduction, for heaven's sake? Why did He have to go and change the system?

As you've probably gathered, our knowledge of the actual 'facts of life', gleaned from our over-protective mothers and grandmothers, was extremely sketchy, Our mothers were probably of the opinion that the less we knew about such matters the better, since all would be revealed to us at the appropriate time by 'Mr. Right' on our wedding night.

Both Cathy and I being fatherless only children, we knew very little about men. We were 'war-time babies'. My father, an RAF pilot, had been killed in a flying mission over Germany, when I was only two years old. Whereas Cathy's father, an American GI, was a bit of mystery in that he was said to have 'gone missing' after being called upon to win the war with the rest of the American troops overseas. He never returned. Cathy's possessive grandparents had not really approved of their daughter's hasty marriage to an American soldier and were in many ways all too delighted that their only daughter and grandchild, Cathy would remain with them in this country after the end of WWII.

Cathy's mother didn't appear to be too bothered by his absence either. According to Cathy there were several 'uncles' who often came to visit, always bringing with them lavish presents of nylon stockings and chocolates. On the rare occasions when I happened to encounter one of these uncles, I could never detect any family resemblance whatsoever to Cathy, her mother or her aging grandparents. But that's families for you, isn't it? Even twins can be remarkably dissimilar in appearance. There were, of course, ugly rumours that GI Goodson had in all likelihood returned to his existing wife and family in the States, but it was something Cathy and I never discussed.

At that stage of our lives, Cathy and I were not really interested in boys, ours being an all-girls school. The enforced weekly attendances for fifth-formers at ballroom dancing classes with the boys from the nearby counterpart grammar school were painful encounters – an ordeal rather than a pleasure. It was my misfortune to be targeted by their powerfully built school captain goal-keeper, who had no sense of rhythm whatsoever. He always made a bee-line for me, then propelled me determinedly round the dance-floor whether it be waltz or foxtrot, his size ten feet crashing cripplingly down on my daintily sandaled toes.

These clumsy, spotty youths fell far short of our ideal partners. No, our ideas of Mr. Right, for whom we were scrupulously preserving our virtue until after the traditional white wedding, were based on the film-star idols of the era – Cary Grant, Rex Harrison, Maurice Chevalier, Charles Boyer – men of the world, slightly greying at the temples, preferably with the hint of a foreign accent. This being the acme of masculine charm, as far as I was concerned. No wonder I fell for Marcus sixteen years my senior, although there was to be no white wedding for me, for reasons I won't go into right now.

Cathy and I couldn't wait to *fall in love* with *the* Mr. Right. Cathy had in fact throughout her adult life fallen in and out of love many times with various Mr. Wrongs, rather than Mr. Rights. I sometimes wondered whether subconsciously she was constantly searching for the father she had never known. Unlike me, I was a one-man woman, but it hadn't put her off men and, if anything, she was even more prolific as a romantic novelist. I just don't know how she found the time for it all.

"And if I can do it, Margot," she had said to me, all those years ago, in that brisk no nonsense way of hers; she'd already completed her seventh romantic novel by then – pure Barbara Cartland, without the pink fluff, "then so can you. Stop feeling sorry for yourself and get writing, girl!"

She was right of course. But it was such hard work at first – much harder than I ever imagined, as you'll probably know if *you*'ve ever tried it. However, I became reasonably successful at what Marcus called 'my little hobby'.

So I hadn't retired by any means, although it was becoming clear that the demand for my kind of writing had greatly diminished, together with the killing-off of children's radio programmes, and the introduction of slick, superficial eye-catching cartoon programmes on children's TV. However, I went on writing regardless, but I really should warn any of you who've been toying with the idea of doing it. Don't get started because you are in danger of becoming hooked and there really is no cure. No, take my advice and stick to being a reader, rather than a writer because it is so much more rewarding.

And now, dear reader, do please read on…

5

After over thirty years in the import and export business for Marcus, first in London then in Saltledale in the North of England, where we'd lived for the past fifteen years, we were still regarded as 'foreigners' by some of the bred-and-born locals, who had a mistrust of anyone moving into their area from soft southern regions.

We, ourselves, however, Marcus and I, had been captivated by the rugged beauty of the Yorkshire hills and dales, right from the outset. Marcus said the forested areas reminded him of the countryside of his childhood. And I, who had never ventured further than Watford Junction until our move northwards, was surprised and delighted that instead finding ourselves surrounded by nothing but cooling towers, smoky chimney and back-to-back houses, soon discovered there were heather-clad moors, pine-forested hills and wild coastal areas to explore. We had come to love the area and pictured ourselves settling there for the rest of our lives.

Retirement came as a great blow to Marcus even though he had already passed the age when most men are all too happy to receive their golden handshakes and devote themselves to those leisure pursuits they had never had enough time for previously.

I could tell Marcus was missing the cut and thrust of the commercial world. He just didn't know what to do with himself now that he was at home all day long. He wandered about the house like a stray dog, always under my feet and getting on my nerves from day one. As one of the ladies of *Cranford* observed, according to Mrs. Gaskell, "A man is *so* in the way in the house!"

Marcus would come wandering into my work-space in the corner of the sitting room and hover over me as I sat gazing out of the window at the garden, turning ideas over in my mind before committing them to paper.

"How about a cup of coffee?" he'd say, which of course meant he would like coffee and would I come to the kitchen and make it.

In the small country East Prussian town where Marcus had been born, he'd been brought up to think wives should observe the three 'k's – kirchen, kuchen and kinder', (church, food and children). The emphasis in our marriage now being on the middle 'k'. It's odd, isn't it, when you come to think about it that such archaic attitudes, no doubt subconsciously absorbed by him in his early life in that part of Germany which no longer exists, being now part of Russia, should still influence his way of thinking. But, I was more than willing to make allowances for this because of the dreadful upheavals he had undergone in his childhood. As his wife, I felt I somehow had to make up to him for the wrongs he had had to suffer. I was, after all, all the family he now had. And it was up to me to heal those past wounds with all the love I had promised to give when we took our marriage vows together.

There was nothing left from his childhood. Everything had been taken away from him. His home, his family, his possessions. Although, there were some things that can never be taken away from a person. Marcus's love of learning and his love of music for instance, remained with him throughout his life. If circumstances had been different, I suppose he might have followed an academic career in the country of his birth, but that was not possible under the strict laws introduced by the

Nazi government in the 1930. Anyone considered to be 'non-Aryan' was prohibited from studying for, or embarking upon, a career in public office or in any of the professions, such as the law, medicine and dentistry.

I've tried to picture Marcus as a boy arriving in this country, having nothing with him apart from a small suitcase of clothing, hurriedly packed by his mother. All he had was one snapshot photo of her taken on the day he left and just five shillings in his pocket. A stranger in a foreign land. And yet, he said that he always considered he was one of the 'lucky ones', escaping to this country from Nazi Germany, almost on the eve of World War II, aboard one of the *Kindertransport* vessels. As he somewhat jokingly described himself, "I was a very elderly '*kind*'." Others being shipped away from their parents and their homeland were mere babes in arms.

Marcus's parents, desperate to save the life of their much loved only child, had somehow managed to get official documents allowing him to leave Germany, on the grounds that he would be studying horticulture here and subsequently work in one of the colonies. And so, he and his parents parted, not knowing when they would see one another again. Soon, they, too, were sent on a journey. Their journey was to Auschwitz, from which they would never return.

It was difficult to persuade Marcus to talk about his early life but I gleaned that his horticultural training in this country, working on a Yorkshire dairy farm was all too brief. It was cut short when he, and some two thousand other refugees from Nazi Germany to this country were mistakenly suspected of being enemy aliens. They were bundled off to Australia aboard a rusty old troop ship, sailing through torpedo-infested waters. A painful experience which some tormented souls did not survive. So I could well understand why Marcus never really wanted to talk about that sad time.

It was indeed fortunate for those who survived that His Majesty's government finally realised they had mistakenly exiled some of our most loyal would-be citizens. Arrangements were hastily made for them to return to this country. And, in a further act of generosity, they were allowed to prove their allegiance to King and country by enlisting in the Allied forces. Mainly in unarmed units such as the Pioneer Corps, just in case they turned out to be spies after all.

"Some of us were sent over to France to take part in the evacuation of Dunkirk," Marcus once told me on one of the rare occasions when he was prepared to talk about his Army days in the Pioneer Corps.

"And then what happened?"

"After that, we were in London during the Blitz, clearing up the damage and destruction. And at the end of the war, we German speakers in the British army were recruited to act as translators at the Nuremberg War Crimes trials."

I was most impressed by the thought that Marcus had performed an important part in bringing some of these criminals to justice. But he shrugged this off by saying,

" Oh *Liebschen*, if you could have seen them! Most of them, when seen in the clear light of day, were pathetic creatures, having allowed themselves to be deluded by so much evil propaganda," adding, "and, of course, after the war, hardly anyone confessed to having been a Nazi. I sometimes wondered where they all suddenly vanished to!"

Having survived the war and served in the armed forces, Marcus was rewarded by being granted British citizenship. And then all in Fate's good time, Marcus and I were brought together, but more of this later.

Now, apart from his interest in classical music, particularly listening to opera whenever the opportunity arose, Marcus was a man without hobbies, other than being a one-time stamp collector. And, this may sound strange to you, he was fascinated by anything to do with cheese. This was probably the outcome of having worked all too briefly soon after his arrival in this country on the Yorkshire dairy farm where he was introduced to the process of cheese-making. In fact, he could hold forth for hours about cheese-making, until I sometimes felt like murdering him.

That's why I feel so guilty about his 'accident'. I just couldn't help feeling that it would never have happened if I hadn't come up with what I thought was a wonderful idea, one morning in late October.

It was one of those Indian summer kind of days you get in that part of northern England, when the heather is in full bloom on the moors and before the harsh winter with its bitter north-eastern winds begins to chill you through and through to the bone. Sunshine was streaming in through the kitchen window. We were just finishing breakfast, to the strains of Vaughan William's *Lark Ascending*, softly playing on the radio, in the background. I was impatient to get to my typewriter to try out my latest ideas for a story about a magical piano.

"What are you going to do with yourself today, darling?" I asked Marcus.

"Read the newspaper. Listen to some music on the radio…" he sighed heavily and shrugged; "I don't know. It's easy enough for you, you have your little hobby to keep you busy."

I could see he was getting depressed and I was worried.

"Well why don't **you** write about something, Marcus?"

"What for instance? And don't say children's stories. And, have you forgotten, my childhood was very different to yours. So it's not really my scene."

Remembering how he had once told me of summer family outings in the woods, birthday parties with friends, and of horse-drawn sleigh rides, sledging and skating on magical white winter days when the lakes froze over, and of being taken to *Hansel and Gretel* at a very young age, I said,

"But you *could* write about your early childhood because it was so different and..."

"No!"

I quickly realised my mistake. It was a painful subject and would be opening up old wounds for him – the loss of his family and most of his childhood friends...How could I, from my own narrow, middle-class background even begin to imagine what it was like when the dark clouds of Nazism descended over Europe, disrupting and destroying family life and families. How stupid of me to even think he would wish to expose his innermost hurts to the world at large! So I quickly said,

"Then something that really interests you. What about...*oh I don't know...cheese,* for instance. You know so much about that. You could write about it. How it's made, where it's made – different kinds, different uses, recipes, folklore. There are endless possibilities. You'll really enjoy researching the background. We're lucky to have such a good reference library here."

"Hmm!"

At least he was thinking about it. That was a good sign.

"And," I added for good measure, "there must be lots of people out there who'd welcome a book on the subject."

How could I have been such a liar! It was only a white lie, I told myself at the time not some enormous whopper for which God may never forgive me but what's He going to think now when He looks at all the havoc it caused? I shudder to think what kind of reception I'm going to get when I turn up at the Pearly Gates.

Oddly enough, throughout the weeks that followed my fateful suggestion, Marcus took with great enthusiasm to researching everything to do with cheese. It was all going so well…too well. One should always be suspicious when Life is too trouble-free, there's bound to be something unpleasant waiting to happen just around the next corner. And there was.

6

I'm sure you can well imagine, without my having to go into all the gory details, the effect that cheese had on poor Marcus, especially if you're a regular viewer of those TV programmes which portray so graphically acts of violence and sudden death; cameras lingering lovingly over realistically simulated grisly injuries and battered corpses.

Actually, Marcus was not killed instantly by the blow on his head. The incident was not witnessed by anyone other than a certain Arthur Blenkinsop, who just happened to be there with his dog, Scruff at that time, or so he claimed.

He claimed that he 'just happened' to be standing at the far end of Friargate Passage by one of those attractively old-fashioned lamp-posts, which enhance that area with an air of Dickensian charm, but which, however, provide very little real illumination on dark winter afternoons.

It was Scruff's favourite place to 'commune with Nature', was how Arthur Blenkinsop so delicately put it, when he was giving his somewhat selective recollection of the 'accident' – Marcus's, of course, not Scruff's.

Arthur Blenkinsop gave me a very garbled account of what had happened when I first encountered him at the hospital. I really couldn't take it all in at that time. From what I could gather, Marcus had been struck on the head by some kind of mysterious foreign object which had fallen from above. It was only much later, a long time after the event in fact, that I found out rather more about that murderous cheese.

I was also to find out later that Arthur Blenkinsop was not only an unreliable witness but a person not to be trusted on other counts as well. What was he really doing there? And why did he inflict that particular daily route march through Friargate Passage on his long-suffering dog instead of taking him along the grassy tree-lined Meadow Tree Walk?

7

Arthur Blenkinsop had reluctantly dragged himself out of bed that morning. Had it not been for Scruff constantly whining and impatiently scratching at the bedroom door, he would not have bothered to get up at all. After all, there was no need for him to do so now. *She,* Ethel, wasn't there any more, prodding him insistently in the back with her bony big toe before he was properly awake. That was her usual way of demanding her early morning cup of tea. At least he didn't have to do that any longer, he told himself. All those years they'd been together and scarcely a word of thanks from her to him for this act of self-sacrifice on his part.

She'd never really appreciated him, he told himself. After all he'd done for her! He'd married her and made an honest woman of her, hadn't he? The ungrateful bitch! Day after day, sitting bolt upright in bed, sipping her tea, her hair in curlers, completely encased in one of those passion-killer nightdresses she always wore. He'd almost forgotten what lay hidden beneath. Not that he had had any inclination to find out of late. As far as he was concerned, the spark of whatever it was that had brought about the conception of their one and only offspring, a daughter by the name of Sharon, and a hastily arranged marriage, had died out some time ago.

Sharon was thirty-something now. She took after her mother to a great extent but Ethel was so possessive, he always felt that he and Sharon had never had a chance to develop a close

33

relationship. So that when Sharon and that bloke she'd met over the internet, her new 'partner' – oh yes, no need nowadays for this generation to be pressurised into marriage, he thought somewhat enviously, when Sharon had emigrated to Australia to be with that bloke, Arthur couldn't really honestly say that he missed her, although Ethel obviously did. Sharon had always been a drain on his pocket, even before she was born. What with the white wedding, and the fancy christening a few months later.

Prior to those happy events, the tearful, heavily pregnant teenaged Ethel had insisted on naming the expected baby:

'Sharon, Hetty, Agnes, Gertrude, that's if it's a girl."

"Why not just Sharon?"

Arthur had always hated the name 'Gertrude' for no other reason than that he had not really taken to *Hamlet* when he had had to study Shakespeare at an all-boys grammar school. Not that he disliked Shakespeare per se.

No, some of the Bard's plays he quite liked. *Othello*, for instance he wouldn't have minded playing the part of Othello, provided his enemy, a form-mate and teacher's pet called Faulkner, was playing Desdemona. Arthur would really have enjoyed putting out *his* light. But it had been Arthur's misfortune to be chosen to read the part of Gertrude, Hamlet's mother, at a time when his voice was breaking and his form-mates were tittering all round him. It brought him out in goose-pimples of shame even to think about it all these years later.

"She's going to be called after my great aunt. I promised her that's why," Ethel had insisted. "She's my godmother and she's got loads of money. Always saying she'd leave it all to me when she passed on. She can't last for ever and she's got no one else to leave it to except me and my baby."

Arthur, somewhat shocked at this hitherto hidden mercenary side of his future bride and mother-to-be of his child, protested feebly over the unfortunate acronym so formed by this particular combination of first names. Ethel, however, had been adamant.

"That's just your dirty mind," she'd sobbed. "It's all your fault. My dad said so. He said you were to blame for everything. Which is why we've got to get married now. And my dad can be real nasty when the mood takes him. Remember? And I'm not changing *my* mind just to please you!"

"But sweetheart," the youthful Arthur had tried to reason with her, "what if it's a boy? We can't call *him* Hetty, Agnes, Gertrude, after your old aunt, can we?"

"I don't care!" Ethel's voice was shrill, with a hysterical edge to it. "Call him anything you like. It's all *your* fault. Landing me with this baby! And, in any case, I'm sure it's going to be a girl. So there!"

Ethel had been beyond reasoning with. So Arthur sheepishly agreed with her.

It was just the same when Sharon reached school age. The local primary school wasn't good enough for her precious Sharon. Oh no! She might pick up nits and bad language there. It had to be private education all the way through, regardless of the expense, which Arthur couldn't really afford. Not on the meagre salary Bowyers Pharmaceuticals paid him.

Then it was that pricey secretarial college. And after that, *her* expensive white wedding, rapidly followed by an even more costly divorce. There seemed to be no end to it as far as Arthur was concerned until now. He fervently hoped that at last Sharon was now far enough away for her to be someone else's financial liability henceforth.

Ethel, however, missed her daughter terribly. There was such a strong bond between them. "More like sisters," Ethel was in the habit of saying, gazing fondly at Sharon, who was indeed growing up to resemble her mother very closely in so many ways. Time and time again since Sharon's departure, Ethel repeatedly expressed her heartfelt wish to go to Australia to be with her beloved daughter.

"And then what would you do, if I weren't here?" she would demand of Arthur. "How would you manage all on your own?"

A question which he didn't dare to answer, his mind being filled with so many delightful possibilities.

So, he was really glad now that Ethel wasn't there any more. At least, that's what he kept telling himself to quell those sudden fleeting feelings of guilt. Although, he had to admit that her departure had happened rather more suddenly than he had anticipated. He could truthfully say, however, that it was the one and only time he had ever hit her and, that at the time, he had no idea it would have such dire consequences.

It was not long after he'd been made redundant from his job in the Accounts Department of Bowyers Pharmaceuticals. Three weeks before Christmas too. How could they do that to him, after he'd been slaving away all those years, balancing their books for them?

"Down-sizing" they called it. Well it had certainly made *him* feel small. Useless. Scrap-heap material, because no one was going to employ him at the age he was now, were they? And Ethel, who'd taken up religion soon after she and Arthur were wed, had made him feel even smaller by constantly telling him she would pray for him, as she prayed 'for all sinners'. What was the use of that? God wasn't going to give him his job back! It wasn't his fault, was it, that there had been a slump in the Stock Market and Bowyers Pharmaceuticals shareholders had been losing money because Putiteg, their new wonder drug for mature men, had not risen to the dizzy heights predicted after their costly promotional advertising campaign!

She still had a job, she was constantly reminding him. She did temping for the Busy Bees' Secretarial Agency and, because she was one of their most reliable workers, her services had always been much in demand. She had been working more or less full-time, and sometimes overtime too, up until her 'disappearance', that is.

As far as Arthur was concerned, what with Ethel's nagging and his suspicions about her relationship with someone in that office where she was working, or rather, had been working until she disappeared, he had felt utterly wretched. What was she doing when she claimed to be working overtime? She'd been looking so pleased with herself, which wasn't right at all when he felt so miserable.

Arthur suspected her of 'goings-on'. Women got funny ideas at her age, even if she had taken up with religion. You just couldn't trust anyone these days. You never knew what they got up to, or were plotting, behind your back. He felt as if *they* were all against him. Not just Bowyers Pharmaceuticals and Ethel. It was the Government as well, especially that Tony Blair and his lot, letting all those foreigners in to take our jobs away from us. If it wasn't for Scruff, Arthur told himself, life wouldn't be worth living any more.

Things had got so bad, he had to go to the doctor to get something for his nerves.

"Not that those pills will do you any good. Doctors! They don't know anything," Ethel had said sniffily. "You should be out looking for another job, you should, not skulking around here all day. It's not healthy."

Stupid bitch! She didn't understand. There were all sorts of jobs a woman could do but it was different for a man. How could he get another job at his age? What was the point of looking? Initially, he had made a special journey every single day to the library to scan through the 'Situations Vacant' columns in the local papers but now, more recently, he'd been browsing in the Reference section, seeking for books concerned with the Law and the rights of the individual. He had other plans in mind, which would be much more rewarding if he played his cards right.

Anyway, Ethel with her cast-iron constitution had never had much need to call upon the medical profession. No, she put all her trust and faith in the Lord, as she was constantly reminding Arthur.

"You should come to Church with me," she urged him.

She knew perfectly well he hadn't set foot inside a church for the last thirty years. Ethel, on the other hand, spent a great deal of her time at the Church and not just on her knees praying. She was a willing helper with all kinds of other activities which went on there. Arthur never went to any of them and had never troubled himself to find out anything about them.

Ethel's activities had undoubtedly had certain advantages for him. From time to time, whenever she embarked upon a baking session, making batches of cakes, scones and pies for some event or other at the Church, there were always plenty of tea-time treats on their own meal table, for which Ethel insisted they must always say, "Thank you Lord for the good food you have put on our plates this day."

Ethel was a good little cook, he had to admit. He missed her for that. It wasn't much fun getting his own meals, especially when he discovered with some surprise that food in the fridge and the larder did not last for ever and some items turned so unpleasantly green and smelly, he suspected that even the mice would turn up their whiskers at them.

The whole house, in fact, was far less comfortable now than it was when Ethel was there. Not only that, but there was a strong smell of decay, which persisted even after he had, as he thought, removed all traces of its origins.

He thought that some of the neighbours had started giving him funny looks.

That nosey Ruby Kersley from Number 9 went out of her way when he was walking Scruff to enquire pointedly about the health of Mrs. Blenkinsop, as she "hadn't seen her around much lately". He felt uncomfortable. Perhaps she'd been spying on him that night when he'd dumped that great plastic sack into the dust-bin. Nearly did his back in with that, he had. He'd had to go to the doctor for pills for that too. Well, he certainly wasn't going to tell that nosey old cow what had gone on between him and Ethel! Anyway, Ethel and he had always made a point of keeping themselves to themselves.

Ruby Kersley had received his mumbled response that "Ethel's visiting her daughter in Australia", with raised eyebrows and a disbelieving sniff.

"Ought to mind her own business," he fumed to himself, retreating behind his own front door.

He needed something to calm his nerves right now. That was why the doctor had given him those pills. He suddenly remembered he had not taken them yet that morning. He had also not had his own breakfast, although he had made a point of feeding Scruff with that doggy delicacy, Chummy Chunks. The Krispie Krunchie cornflakes packet was empty and the carton of milk, which he had forgotten to put back in the fridge for several days, was solid and smelt more unpleasant than usual. He thought about having some black tea, but he didn't really fancy that.

Then, he spotted at the back of the cupboard, a small bottle of liqueur brandy which had been given them one Christmas by that Ruby Kersley from Number 9. In all probability, it was a present that someone had given to Ruby, whose preference was for 'a nice drop of British sherry' rather than 'fancy foreign liquor'.

Ethel, who was strictly teetotal, had decreed the liqueur brandy must be kept 'for emergency medicinal use only'. Arthur decided this *was* a medical emergency since he urgently needed something to wash down his medicine and possibly cheer him up. It had a rather sickly flavour but it was better than tea without milk.

So, thus fortified, he set off, like a man on a mission later than usual that fateful morning with Scruff in tow to deliver by hand, but as unobtrusively as possible, his latest communication to the offices of Messrs. Smethers and Lybrand.

8

When I came to think about it, *someone* must have had the presence of mind to call an ambulance, which arrived promptly and transferred not just Marcus but Arthur Blenkinsop and his dog, Scruff, as well to the A&E department at the General. I was soon to find out that this *someone* was in fact Arthur Blenkinsop.

Although I did wonder fleetingly how it was that Scruff had been included in these arrangements. Surely it was strictly against regulations for dogs to be transported by ambulance? Maybe he had been bundled into the front seat with the driver, sneaked aboard unnoticed perhaps, or even given a lift to the hospital in a car by some tender-hearted animal lover. Who knows how he'd got there. But he was there all right when I arrived at the A&E.

And that was my first encounter with Scruff and Arthur Blenkinsop. He came cantering across, planted himself down in the chair next to mine as soon as he realised who I was, and announced,

"Came here together. Me and your hubby. After the…the …um…unfortunate occurrence. At full-steam ahead, flashing lights, sirens going and all!"

He seemed to think this had somehow conferred celebrity status on him. I merely nodded, being unable to think of a suitable reply, as I waited in a state of numbed anxiety for news in the casualty-crowded waiting area, while Marcus lay on a hospital trolley in one of the six curtained cubicles, until such time as a bed became available for him in one of the wards.

Again, this piece of information about bed-allocation was conveyed to me by this Arthur Blenkinsop, whom hospital staff members seemed to assume was some kind of close relative of mine.

"Wonderful the way those lady para-medics handle you in an emergency," he confided to me in a loud stage-whisper from which I assumed he must be slightly deaf.

Several heads turned interestedly in our direction, hoping, no doubt, to hear more of the particular emergency which had caused us to be here, and to distract their minds from their own acute pains and sufferings.

He was gazing earnestly at me with bleary blue eyes which I was to come to know all too well. Scruff, stretched out at his feet, on the waiting area floor, had dozed off into that twitchy-snorey way sleeping dogs do.

"It was really very kind of you Mr. Blenkinsop to…to do…what you did…but…" I began, hoping he would take the hint that there was no need for him to stay beside me in such close proximity.

"Oh it's no bother at all. You see, I need to be here myself and please call me 'Arthur' as I expect we'll be seeing a lot more of each other from now on," he said, leering at me with large yellowing teeth and reaching out with his bony fingers to take my hand.

Whatever did he mean about *needing to be here* and *seeing a lot more of each other?* I resented such familiarity from a complete stranger, especially one who had the look of a disappointed also-ran retired race horse.

Then I told myself that I shouldn't be feeling so uncharitable towards this unlikely Good Samaritan. He had, after all, or so he assured me, been the one who made sure Marcus had been brought here to receive prompt medical treatment, whereas others who might have been in the area at the time of the 'occurrence', as he euphemistically put it, must have most likely turned a blind eye and hurried by. All the same, his remarks had added yet further to my state of numbed confusion. I couldn't take in what had happened during the past few hours.

The day when it had all happened had been such a beautiful morning too. At that time of year here, the nights are long and the rosy golden sunrise, only half-seen through sleep-hazed eyes when one wakes in the mornings. It was too early to get out of bed when Marcus and I had woken that morning, so we had snuggled up together in each other's arms, chatting about nothing in particular, until we both agreed it was high time to bestir ourselves. Marcus's retirement was really no excuse for staying in bed. We had things to do, especially Marcus. Now that he had begun researching so enthusiastically this new found interest of his, he spent most of his time at the Central Library.

Nothing could have been further from my mind that day than that something awful was about to happen to Marcus. Not now. Not any more. Tragic events were all part of the past – dead and buried. These were to be our golden years, shared in tranquillity until, as we had vowed to one another, Death should us part at some far-off future date.

So, when that call from the hospital came telling me my husband had had 'an accident' and 'no, it wasn't a car accident nor an attack by a mugger', but to 'come as soon as possible to the Casualty Department' and assuring me 'not to worry', because he was in good hands, I thought there must be some mistake.

That was it! They'd phoned the wrong number – someone with a similar name perhaps. But who else did I know who had such a name? No one. 'Prettiflower' had been the unique name granted to Marcus as a most loyal, naturalized British subject, playing his part in the fight for democratic freedom, after volunteering for the British Armed Forces and upon swearing the Oath of Allegiance to His Majesty, King George the Sixth, His Heirs and Successors. And it is a name I was, and still am, proud to bear until the end of my days.

I had only the briefest of glimpses of a red-blanketed figure, presumably Marcus, lying on a trolley, then being whisked away and into a cubicle, where the curtains were immediately closed.

The seats in the waiting area when I arrived were nearly all occupied by young and old in varying states of distress and discomfort, apart from two perky old ladies in knitted tea-cosy hats, who arrived with a couple of large suitcases, as if they were about to set off on holiday to some winter wonderland. What were they doing here? Shouldn't they be at the bus terminal down the road? They both appeared to be in the best of health as they sat there happily chatting. One of them knitting furiously away at something pink and fluffy. Another tea-cosy hat perhaps?

A television screen dominated one corner, showing one of those inane programmes, punctuated with bursts of hysterical clapping and piped laughter. No one was watching it.

All the while, members of staff were constantly passing backwards and forwards. They all appeared to be too busy, or too important-looking, to be stopped and asked for information, especially those not wearing any kind of uniform but with stethoscopes dangling round their necks.

On arrival, I had been told to take a seat and I would be called in due course. So I waited. Names were called out. Individuals rose and shuffled off, presumably to be put out of their misery. To reassure the waiting fraternity, there was a large notice board informing us that the waiting time would be not more than one hour. So I waited, and waited. I had no idea for how long. I lost all track of time.

It came as something of a surprise when a big-bosomed nurse came bustling along and called out,

"Arthur Blenkinsop. The doctor will see you now."

I was about to ask her if there was any news of Marcus for me but she must have noticed Scruff for the first time. She glared accusingly at me, since Arthur Blenkinsop had already shambled off, presumably for his tête-à-tête with one of the medics.

"Dogs are *not* allowed in here. Out!"

She was glowering so fiercely at Scruff and he was gazing up at me so pathetically, what could I do but meekly take hold of his collar and lead him out through the glass swing doors. Useless for me to protest that he wasn't my dog. Anyway, I didn't want to be absent for too long from the waiting area, in case I was at last summoned to poor Marcus's bedside, or trolley-side, as the case may be.

I hoped there would be some nearby place where Scruff could be tethered, until his master returned. Fortunately, immediately under the Casualty Department window there was a wooden bench where, even in the dusk and cold of that wintry afternoon, smokers sat puffing on, and coughing over, their cigarettes. Smoking, like dogs, was not allowed inside the hospital building. To my great relief, Scruff obligingly flopped down at the carpet-slippered feet of the first smoker and promptly fell asleep again. One less worry, at least, as far as I was concerned.

I was now on the verge of tears and I couldn't have borne it if Scruff had howled non-stop for ages at being parted from his owner, especially as Arthur Blenkinsop had been closeted with one of the stethoscoped-necklaced individuals, one of the junior trainee doctors, for quite some considerable time.

Eventually he emerged from the consulting room, clutching a sheaf of papers and looking very pleased with himself, like a 30-1 horse who'd come in second or third after all.

I was about to hurry down the corridor towards the lift, having at last been informed that Marcus was being admitted to Florence Ward on the second floor when Arthur Blenkinsop came cantering after me and grabbed my arm as I was stepping into the lift. There was the light of battle in his eyes.

"I'm going to sue 'em," he said. "You and your hubby should do so too. Shock – that's what I've got and Scruff too, after what we've been through today. I'll be in touch…"

He was still gabbling away as the lift doors closed. What on earth was he talking about? And why was he going to keep in touch with me? He sounded as if he meant it. It was a most unappealing prospect. It was as if I was in someone else's nightmare from which there was no escape.

9

Charles sighed heavily, looking at the pile of paperwork waiting to be dealt with on his desk. No way would he be able to leave early tonight, or even at a reasonable hour if he was going to tackle that lot. He was strictly against taking work home with him, except on very rare occasions. Most of the files were far too bulky and anyway, it wasn't fair on Sandra or the kids.

That reminded him. He had better ring Sandra now to warn her that he would be late, in case she was planning something special for them this evening. He hated anything over-cooked, or over-done. He was a man who believed in moderation in all things, which is why he felt slight pangs of guilt over last night's over-indulgence. Ah well, he'd better put things right with Sandra when he got home tonight.

Theirs was a good marriage, he mused as he waited for Sandra, or Monique to answer the phone. Nearly fifteen years. Not bad going these days when one in three ended up in the divorce courts.

He and Sandra had met at Law College. He had been amazed that she, the most dazzling redhead he had ever set eyes on *and* marvellous legs to go with it, had singled him out from all that student crowd who'd surrounded her and he'd been bewitched by her. Her crowd had spent more time partying than studying, which is probably why most of them failed the course, including Sandra. Whereas he, having worshipped her from afar, and having missed out on all that wild night-life by ploughing doggedly on with his studies, finally achieved the honour of being able to practice as a fully-fledged solicitor, and of winning Sandra's hand in marriage into the bargain. There were times, even now when he could scarcely believe his good fortune.

Sandra, on her part, was not enamoured with the thought of devoting any more time to her studies in order to retake the more boring aspects of the law. She rejoiced in the rosy prospect of settling down in matrimony with such a reliable partner as Charles, with the promise of a comfortable income and an appealing life-style.

Daddy would be sure to help out initially. She was certain of that. He always had. Ever since she had smiled her first smile and uttered her first words, "dadda...dad... mun... mun...mun...eey...", which had sent him into such raptures of delight, he had opened her first bank account forthwith. This he had topped up freely at frequent intervals and Sandra, not to disappoint her doting father, had drawn upon this account freely and frequently, for 'life's little essential luxuries'.

She had accepted Charles's hesitant proposal of marriage with alacrity. He would make an ideal family solicitor in some country town, where she would, with suitable domestic help, play an active part in local affairs and bring up the four brilliant and beautiful children, which she planned to have, but not too early in the marriage. She'd see to that.

For Sandra, everything had worked out very much according to plan, except that so far there had only been three Hardy children and all girls too. With her biological clock now ticking towards closing time, she had made up her mind it was time for her and Charles to conceive number four, which, of course, would most definitely be a boy.

Charles, however, although he would have liked a son and

heir, was blissfully unaware of what Sandra had in mind for him. He was quite fond of his three daughters now that they had reached the age when, as he sometimes put it to male friends, 'they were almost human'. It was a great relief to him that the era of nights of broken sleep and bawling babies, which he had endured for Sandra's sake, was to a large extent, now a thing of the past.

At long last someone in the Hardy household was answering the phone.

" 'Allo, 'allo, who is that please?"

"Ah, Monique, it's Mr. Hardy. Can I speak to my wife, please?"

"No, monsieur, you cannot. She is not 'ere."

Monique was a girl of few words, especially when she was called upon to answer the phone, which she regarded as not part of her job description. Besides, she was still feeling somewhat out-of-sorts, which is why she had slept in late that morning.

"Hold on, Monique…"

It sounded as if she was about to ring off.

"Just give her a message for me, would you?"

"Yes, yes, what is it please?"

"Tell her I won't be home until late tonight. That's all. Have you got that, Monique?"

"Yes, yes! Bien sûr. Au revoir, Monsieur."

Charles had suddenly remembered that it was Sandra's day for attending one of her voluntary organisations fund-raising events and that she, herself, would probably not be home until later that afternoon. She gave so much of her time, bless her, to organising and attending charity coffee mornings and luncheons, bring-and-buy sales, serving on voluntary committees and so on. She worked so hard. It was remarkable how she fitted it all in as well as managing the household too. He was a very lucky man.

Charles had not remembered, however, that it was also to be Monique's night off after she had put the children to bed. Thus her mind was focused more on her own plans for attending a disco in town with her friends that evening than on the Hardys' domestic arrangements. Having found a scrap of paper by the telephone which had not been scribbled all over by the Hardy children, she hurriedly scrawled a note for Sandra: 'Monsieur Hardy will not be home tonight at all', and propped it up on the kitchen dresser where Sandra would be sure to see it when she came in.

10

"Here's your tea, Mr. Hardy."

"Thank you, Ethel. Just put it down there, would you?"

Why was the woman still hovering around? Not like her at all. Mousy little thing but she was one of the most efficient secretaries he had ever had. Seemed to enjoy the work too. Not like some of the others, who were always impatient to rush off on the dot. No, she didn't seem to mind doing overtime and she'd often bring him a piece of her own home-made delicious cake, carefully wrapped up in a paper lace doily, to have with his cup of tea or coffee.

She'd even coyly placed a vase of flowers on his desk once or twice, until he was forced to point out that it was in danger of being knocked over by the weighty legal files. He thought maybe she had a crush on him. It was rather flattering really. As far as he was aware, none of the other partners at Smethers & Lybrand enjoyed that sort of attention from their secretaries. Pity she was only a temp, filling in while his own secretary was on maternity leave.

Charles glanced up. It wasn't Ethel. It was Amy, the grey-haired gossipy one.

"Sorry, I thought you were Ethel. Isn't she in today?"

"Oh no, Mr. Hardy. Ethel's left. Quite suddenly, as a matter of fact. She hasn't been in since Christmas. I expect the Agency will be sending us someone else soon."

This was said with some relish. Ethel was not particularly

well liked by the other secretaries. She wouldn't be drawn on anything concerning her own private life, or other people's for that matter. She showed no interest in the girlie office chit-chat *and* she had even been seen to be reading a bible of all things in their lunch break, when the others in the office were absorbed in their pages of *Hello* magazine or a Catherine Cookson saga. It was whispered, behind her back, of course, that she had a 'thing' about Charles Hardy, from the way she looked whenever his name was mentioned.

"So I'll be looking after you now, Mr. Hardy," Amy told Charles, bestowing on him a motherly smile and, before Charles could recover from this dismaying piece of news, she went on,

"Wasn't it awful about that accident. Almost on our doorstep too. Poor man being hit on the head like that! Someone said it was a flying missile from Outer Space. But I can't believe that, can you? Nobody actually saw what happened, except for that peculiar man who's often hanging around here with his dog. You don't suppose that cheese had anything to do with it, do you, Mr. Hardy?"

Charles, who had not really been listening to any of this, apart from the last few words and, having completely dismissed the offensive cheese from his mind when he consigned it to the second-floor balcony, said in his most authoritative voice,

"Most unlikely! So, Amy perhaps you could...?"

She was off again before he had completed the sentence.

"The ambulance got here ever so quickly. But I do hope he'll be all right, don't you?"

"Yes, yes. Of course. Amy would you *please* get your notebook so we can start work right away."

As the door closed behind her, Charles suddenly recalled with some unease his action over that obnoxious cheese. *Could* that have had anything to do with the unfortunate accident?

Surely not! Nevertheless, he supposed he would have to make some further enquiries into the matter, or get one of the secretaries to do it for him later. But work must come first. He hastily scribbled 'accident victim' in capital letters on his memo pad underneath the earlier note he had made to order flowers for Sandra.

Ah, that reminded him, this *was* a matter requiring urgent attention. By the time he left the office that evening, Floribunda, the florist across the way, would be closed. As soon as Amy returned with her notepad, he must tell her to deal immediately with the ordering of flowers for his wife.

★★★

Amy, weighed down with a mountain of papers all requiring urgent action, returned to the secretaries' office just as the others were switching off their word processors, putting on their make-up, donning their winter coats, boots and scarves and gathering up their shopping bags, ready to depart. She was somewhat piqued that she was the one to be lumbered with all this extra work, while others could go rushing off home to be with their husbands and children, or tart themselves up for an evening out with boyfriends. True *she* didn't have a husband at home to return to, only her tabby cat, Tibbles, but that was no excuse for them to leave everything to her.

She picked upon Carol, the office junior, who, in Amy's eyes, was a rather dozy young madam and who had yet to prove her worth to Smethers and Lybrand.

"Carol," she said, in an 'I'll-not-take-no-for-an-answer' voice, "Mr. Hardy wants you to order some flowers urgently for him. Run along now to Floribunda before they close. Go on. Hurry."

Carol, whose thoughts were preoccupied with what she should wear when she met up with her new boyfriend that evening and how much cleavage she should reveal on a first date, with an ice-cold north-easterly wind blowing, stared back at Amy uncomprehendingly.

Amy hurriedly thrust Charles' memo into Carol's hands, at the same time propelled her determinedly towards the door.

"They'll most likely arrange special delivery tonight, if you ask them nicely. They know where and what to send," she added kindly, noting the look of bewilderment on Carol's face, "and there's no need to come back to the office afterwards. I'm sure you'll be wanting to be meeting your boyfriend after work. So, you run along and enjoy yourself. *I* shall be the only one working late tonight."

The air of martyrdom which accompanied this last remark was ignored by the others, as they all murmured hasty condolences and trouped out of the office.

★★★

A somewhat confused and breathless Carol arrived on the doorstep of Floribunda, just as the 'closed ' sign was about to be hung on the door. A wan and wilted-looking florist opened the door. She was exhausted. She had been up since the early hours that morning, working single-handed, her assistant having gone down with an ill-timed attack of flu. This was always their busiest time, apart from St. Valentine's Day and Mother's Day and that one-off fever of activity, a while ago, when overwhelming demands were made for floral tributes for Princess Diana's funeral. At least that had been in the summer, when supplies of flowers were plentiful.

It was now, in these sad dark post-Christmas and early New Year days, when it was most difficult of all to keep up with requests which came pouring in for funeral wreaths and tasteful floral tributes. Every one of them had to be delivered to exactly the right place at exactly the right time too, especially for cremations. Today had been one of the worst days ever. She hadn't even had time to stop for a sandwich or make herself a mug of hot 'cup-a-soup'.

The florist's cold fingers ached. Her whole body ached. She was probably going down with flu too. But, she was a lady with a big heart and one look at Carol's troubled face convinced her that here was another grief-stricken soul, whose garbled plea for the urgent dispatch of a floral tribute, had to be dealt with right away. Gently she took the crumpled note which Carol held out to her.

"They told me to say it's urgent and you'd know where and what to send. It's all written down on the note," Carol said breathlessly.

The number 16 bus was due at any moment. Carol did not want to miss it and have to hang around in the cold for another half an hour. She'd be late for her date.

"All right, I'll see to it myself, right away. Don't worry, my dear. You run along. I can see you're in a hurry."

Carol, having thus discharged her out-of-hours duties for Smethers and Lybrand so satisfactorily, was out of the shop and racing off like an Olympic runner to the corner of the market square to catch her bus, while the florist was still searching around for her reading glasses among the debris of discarded leaves and fallen flower petals on her work-bench, in order to take in fully the details of this last-minute assignment.

"Oh my God!" she gasped as she read the crumpled note. "Not that nice Mr. Hardy from the solicitors' offices further down the Passage!"

From her workroom at the back of the shop, she had hardly been aware of the dramatic events which had taken place in Friargate Passage earlier that afternoon. Until, that is, Rupert Brooke-Smythe from the bookshop next door, always one for recounting grisly tales, had popped his head round the door to tell her some incredible story about a man having been fatally injured by a flying missile, outside the offices of Messrs. Smethers and Lybrand around lunch-time that morning.

No, Rupert had said, he didn't know who it was or what it was exactly which had struck the fatal blow. It could have been anyone or anything. The victim was probably one of those legal eagles who worked there, on his way out for a late lunch, Rupert supposed, before returning to his book shop and leaving her to get on with a magnificent and intricate tribute of white carnations and laurel leaves, she was working on for the funeral of someone's 'Great Mum'.

So, Rupert had been right about it being one of the lawyers from Smethers & Lybrand! It must have been Mr. Hardy then! Such a lovely man too. He reminded her of that film star, Rex Harrison. And he, Mr. Hardy, that is, always sent his wife such beautiful bouquets for their anniversaries. Oh how sad. His poor wife and family. How terrible for them!

Why was it that bad things always happened to good people? She'd seen so much of it throughout her working life. All those funeral floral tributes she'd so superbly contrived confirmed this belief.

No wonder that poor young girl who'd brought the message looked so upset. She must be one of the secretaries from poor Mr. Hardy's offices.

The instructions on the crumpled note, which had been thoughtfully written in capitals because the secretaries always complained they couldn't read Charles's handwriting, read: 'Send flowers to Mrs. Hardy' then underneath, also in capitals, and as far as she could make out the words 'accident victim'. How good of them at Smethers and Lybrand to have acted so promptly and to think of sending flowers straight away to Mrs. Hardy! What a touching gesture. A very tactful way of preparing her for bad news.

Flowers, in their silent beauty spoke a language of their

own to convey messages of comfort, love and joy. Tired though she was, she would create a most tasteful bouquet in memory of Mr. Hardy. A pity she had used up all the carnations in the tribute to 'A Great Mum' but there were those Madonna lilies and laurel leaves left over from her labours earlier that day.

Bouquets were so much better than wreathes because they could be passed on after the funeral to cheer up the long-stay patients in the geriatric ward at the General Hospital. She set to work with skilful fingers, and then searched around for one of her special cards with a suitable message printed on it, to accompany the bouquet, which she would deliver personally to poor Mrs. Hardy that same evening.

11

They couldn't have been kinder – those nurses at the General Hospital, when they broke the news to me. They offered me a cup of tea and asked if there was any one I would like to contact to be with me now that Marcus had gone. Was there any family member, a daughter or a son, perhaps? So that I wouldn't be on my own.

Apart from Esther, that neurotic distant cousin of Marcus, there was, of course, no one. She was, after all, Marcus's only surviving relative, but she and I had never been close. Up until a few hours ago there had been Marcus *and* me. We had been everything to each other. And now, just me – alone. But I wasn't going to say that. It's not something you care to admit to other people when, like me, you've reached a certain age. It makes you sound so pathetic, like an outcast from society.

"I've very good neighbours," I told them. Although, if they'd asked me to name any of them, I'd have been hard put to bring any of their names to my benumbed mind at that moment.

That's the trouble with being 'detached' rather than 'semi-' in a somewhat rural setting. Half an acre of garden separated us from our nearest neighbours in Grandby Lane and I'd always been too busy with my writing to indulge in their regular round of coffee mornings, charity lunches and bridge-playing afternoons, which formed an important part in the social lives of most of the other women living there and forged a bond between them. The long-term residents, that is. They mostly belonged to the conservative, C of E, cashmere sweater and pearls brigade. I just didn't fit. In their eyes, Marcus and I were both 'foreigners' and anyway, I'd soon found these social events almost as uncomfortable as the enforced dinner parties with Marcus's colleagues and their wives.

There were other women who were comparative newcomers to Granby Lane when their managerial husbands had been moved by their industrial companies into the area. On those rare occasions when I met them, I could see they were also somewhat ill-at-ease among the residents of long standing. Although they tried hard not to show it, they were obviously home-sick for their London suburban lifestyle, south of Watford and longing to be repatriated back to their former homeland, at the earliest opportunity.

However, when Marcus and I moved here some fifteen years ago from the overcrowded hustle and bustle of a London suburb and a postage-stamp garden, to this hamlet on the outskirts of the industrial complex that dominates the Northcaster area, we had fallen in love with our mock Tudor half-timbered residence, nestling among mature conifers, evergreens and deciduous trees – trailing weeping willows and deceptively delicate silver birches. In spring, there were carpets of daffodils under the trees. There were rose beds in the garden too, thriving in the heavy clay soil of this area. The trees reminded Marcus of the forests of his youth, and the roses were my special delight. They were rich in colour and fragrance in the summer. Beyond the garden, we could just catch glimpses of distant hilltops, blue-green in summer and snow-capped in winter. *This* was where we would end our working days and then live out the rest of our lives in golden tranquillity. Little did we dream Fate had other plans in store for us.

"I've an old friend who will come and stay with me," I

said, as sudden inspiration struck me. Who better than Cathy Goodson at a time like this?

In the semi-rural London suburb where Cathy and I had grown up together, Cathy's grandfather and his father before him, had been the local undertakers, or funeral directors as they are called now. There were stables at the back of their house where two fine black stallions, immaculately groomed and bearing black plumes upon their noble heads, had once been used to pull a magnificent hearse, with plate glass windows and shiny brass fittings. Cathy's grandfather would proudly show us pictures of splendid funereal occasions of former times, and sigh at the memory of those good old days when men and boys would doff their hats and everyone stood in respectful silence along the highway, as the cortege passed by.

Cathy and I used to fantasize about being transported in that beautiful carriage, in a glass coffin surrounded by flowers but, like the Sleeping Beauty, being awakened by a kiss from a handsome Prince in the nick of time. No kiss of mine could awaken my beloved Marcus now. Not now that he had closed his eyes upon this world for ever.

The thought of this overwhelmed me. Faust gave his immortal soul for extra years of life which he squandered away. What wouldn't I give for just a few moments to share with Marcus now, so that I could tell him how much I loved him! But such things can only happen in fiction and one cannot turn fiction into reality. That was an undeniable fact and I must face up to reality.

It was indeed fortunate that Cathy was my friend and that she, being between love affairs, would be able to come right away.

"I'll be with you in a couple of hours," she assured me, when I telephoned her before I left the hospital.

Her voice was warm and comforting although she was

naturally shocked and saddened by my news. There had always been a soft spot in her heart for Marcus, among the other many loves of her life. I was relieved that she hadn't asked for details of his sudden death. She had probably assumed it was from natural causes such as a heart attack and I couldn't yet bring myself to talk about his unfortunate accident. In any case, I was not, at that time, fully aware of all that had happened, having not fully grasped even the sketchiest of details provided by that strange dog-man at the hospital. I could tell her later – much later, but not now.

There were, of course, others who had to be told, as well as Marcus's distant cousin, Esther. There were his former business colleagues. They would need to know about the funeral arrangements. For Cathy, from her childhood background, death was a perfectly natural subject to talk about. So with her practical common-sense, she would help me in making all the necessary arrangements because I had no idea where to begin.

I don't know how you're supposed to know what has to be done when a death, especially an unexpected one like Marcus's, occurs – making all the funeral arrangements and that sort of thing. There are no lessons taught in schools and it's not a subject for polite conversation at dinner parties, coffee mornings or, indeed any other social function now, is it? Although, of course, death and disaster are popular subjects with our present-day media. Our daily newspapers and TV programmes are full of them. But then these events don't usually involve people we know personally, do they?

I suppose we all think we ourselves are immortal these days. It's never going to happen to *us*, only to other people. It's the taboo subject of the twentieth/twenty-first century in polite society. 'Sex', 'condoms', 'periods' are no longer the whispered words they once were. They frequently appear now in the media amongst all the other advertisements designed to persuade us to spare no expense to be everlastingly young, beautiful and desirable to the opposite sex and have fun, fun, fun. As yet, there are no funeral directors ads on TV, are there? I really think that there should be.

I could hear the phone ringing and ringing as I unlocked the front door when I returned home that evening. The hall was shrouded in darkness. I rushed across to grab up the telephone receiver and tripped over the vacuum cleaner, which I'd left standing there earlier that day, in my haste to get to Marcus at the hospital.

"Mrs. Prettiflower?"

"Y-e-s?"

It was a voice I didn't recognise. He had a slightly slurred northern intonation.

"We met today at the hospital. It's Arthur Blenkinsop. Said I'd be in touch. Remember?"

Him! Oh my God! That strange, shabby also-ran, with the bleary blue-eyes. The one at the hospital with the scruffy dog. What on earth did he want at a time like this? Dazed, and now bruised from my encounter with the vacuum cleaner, all I could say was a wary "Yes?" again.

"I think you and I, and your hubby of course, if he's up to it, should get together to sue for damages from those bloody lawyers…if you'll excuse the expression. But that's what they are! You can't trust 'em. Any of 'em. I could tell you a thing or two about them. Always up to things behind your back. Oh and by the way, how is he, your hubby, I mean?" he added, by way of an afterthought.

"He's dead," I said and put the phone down.

I had no idea what he was talking about. What did he mean about 'lawyers' and 'suing them'? Why would I want to sue anybody? What would be the point of that That wouldn't bring Marcus back to me, would it? How insensitive can you be?

I wondered fleetingly if he would have the nerve to ring back, saying he had been cut off. So I left the phone off the hook and stumbled shakily into the kitchen to put the kettle on.

What creatures of habit we are! It was only as I poured the boiling water into the tea-pot, I realised what I had done without thinking. I had set out on the tea-tray our two '*Thine*' and '*Mine*' mugs, impulse buys Marcus and I had made one sunny afternoon from a local market stall. Then bleak reality suddenly struck home.

He and I would never again be sharing those companionable moments here in this kitchen, sipping our tea together, with music on the radio softly playing in the background. I sank down on the nearest chair and for the first time that day wept, letting my pent-up tears flow and flow.

Then I must have dozed off. The doorbell was ringing with stinging insistence. The entire house was in complete darkness and my pot of tea was stone-cold.

"God, you look awful!" was Cathy's greeting. "By the way, your phone's out of order. I tried to reach you several times from motorway service stations. And, what *are* you doing in the dark?"

She switched on all the lights, put the phone back in place and then put her arms round me in a warm, comforting hug. For the moment at least, I felt much, much better.

Cathy, herself, now a glowing honey blonde, and in a stunning black outfit, was looking marvellous, considering she had recently separated from the latest love of her life. She always was skinny so she could carry off to perfection whatever clothes she chose to wear. She ordered me to sit down while she busied herself around the kitchen, boiling the kettle and refilling the teapot.

Over a freshly made pot of tea, she persuaded me to tell

her about Marcus's accident. So I told her all I knew at that time was that he had been struck on the head by some unknown object falling out of the blue.

"Aeschylus syndrome!" She exclaimed.

"Cathy, what on earth are you talking about?"

Then she explained what this meant. Cathy was a great reader as well as a prolific writer. She was a walking encyclopaedia on the subject of literature, ancient and modern. She knew all about that unfortunate Greek dramatist with the bald head and his fatal encounter with the tortoise.

"Sounds better than 'hit on the head by an unknown falling 'whatever-it-was'. Don't you think so, duckie?"

I nodded. It had a dignified ring to it.

"So that's what you tell 'em. Anyone who's nosey enough to ask."

I knew Marcus's distant cousin, Esther, was sure to ask, because of her obsession with matters relating to health, or rather sickness.

"Yes, but what d'you think I should do about this weird dog-man, this Arthur Blenkinsop?"

"Oh don't bother about *him*," she said dismissively. "He sounds like a right crank anyway. And, you've got other things to see to right now, after you've had some rest."

I meekly agreed. I was exhausted but even so, that night and the nights that followed, I was unable to get much sleep at all.

It was Cathy, bless her, who from Marcus's meticulously kept address book, made out lists of people to notify and, over the next few days, it was Cathy who attended to most of the arrangements to give Marcus a memorable send-off.

"But *you'll* have to speak to that cousin of Marcus, Esteria, or whatever her name is."

"Esther," I corrected her.

I knew that Cathy knew perfectly well what Esther was called and that this was her way of distancing herself from this particular task. I wasn't looking forward to it either. I was dreading it. I never enjoyed talking to Esther at the best of times because she never seemed to listen to anything I said. I felt she'd never really approved of Marcus marrying me in the first place.

"Why couldn't he had found himself some nice Jewish girl? Why did he have to go and marry 'out'?"

Esther had, no doubt, voiced this concern many times over to her fellow members of the Ladies Circle at her local synagogue, where such disasters were most probably freely aired, along with her most recent ailments, real and imaginary. Esther and her husband, Bernie, were both regular attendees at the synagogue, close to Bernie's prosperous dental practice in north London. They had no children, only a very pampered poodle dog, who never went out in the Park or on the Heath on chilly days without its designer doggy jacket.

Marcus had been surprised by, and uncomfortable with, Esther's reaffirmation of Judaism. He, himself, had no such leanings in that direction. For him it was sufficient to believe in the power of music, poetry and art to nourish his soul, in preparation for the life beyond. It was, in fact, his love of music which he taught me to share which had brought us together in the first place.

"Our parents, Esther's and mine," Marcus once explained to me, "were never that much concerned with their Jewish identity. They were cultured people who loved the paintings of artists like Lovis Corinth, Gustav Klimt and Franz Marc; the works of Goethe and Schiller; and music, especially the music of Beethoven, Mozart and Schubert.

They took me to my first opera, the wonderful fairy tale of *Hansel and Gretel* when I was just five years old. You see, they thought of themselves primarily as Germans, and were proud to be so. Until that is, Hitler came to power and then—" he sighed and shrugged, "—and then…everything changed."

It was too painful to go into more detail. It was his way of coping with the past to erase it from his memory.

Maybe Esther's insistence on her Jewishness was because she somehow felt she owed it now to her parents to do so. It was her way of honouring their memory. I often wondered what it must have been like for her, and other children like her, to lose every meaningful thing in their lives at such a young age. Those they loved and who loved them. And then to lose their sense of identity and of belonging, spurned by the country of their birth and facing an unknown future in a foreign land.

Esther's parents made arrangements for her escape from Berlin soon after the 'spontaneous' acts of desecration and destruction of Kristallnacht, when the smashing of glass, the splintering of wood and the cries of terror echoed through the city streets. Esther's parents did not escape the attention of the Nazis. Their home and all their belongings were seized and they, like Marcus's parents, died in Auschwitz.

When Esther first arrived in this country, she was sent to a hostel in Oxford and allowed to work as a domestic servant until she was able to train as a nurse at one of the London teaching hospitals, which is where she met Bernie, when he was a student there. As a domestic servant, the work was back-breakingly hard, from all accounts. It must have been a great shock to the system for one who had been raised by loving parents in a comfortable well-to-do doctor's household, staffed with a maid and a nanny for Esther.

In all fairness to her, I knew Esther loved Marcus too, in her own way. They were the only survivors of that family, and so she had a right to know what had happened to Marcus.

But, it is so difficult to bear the grief of others when your own heart is heavy with sorrow, apart from anything else. The worst part of all would be having to tell her that a cremation and a non-religious service was being planned.

She was stunned by the news of Marcus's death, of course. But, being the hypochondriac that she was, she wanted to know more about the cause of Marcus's death.

"This Ashy…whatever syndrome you say he died of? I do not know of it. Is it contagious?" she asked anxiously. "Is it hereditary?"

"No, no! Not at all, Esther," I reassured her. "It was very sudden and I was told he did not suffer." Then, taking a deep breath I said, "Now, about the funeral…"

As I suspected, she was shocked beyond words that it was to be a cremation, which to her way of thinking was immoral.

She would be thinking, "How can you be ready to meet your Maker at the Second Coming if you are nothing more than a pile of ashes?" Although, it's my opinion, that if God created Adam from a handful of dust, then surely He would have no problem reassembling my darling Marcus from the ashes.

To soften the blow, I said, "Marcus's favourite music will be played during the service and there will be that beautiful *Requiem* by Mozart. Remember how he loved Mozart?"

I could hear Bernie, whose views were more liberal than hers in these matters, in the background, trying to be helpful with alternative suggestions relating to Golders Green Crematorium, pointing out that it was the last resting place of many hallowed names such as Sigmund Freud, Wolf Mankowitz and Conrad Veidt. Surely Bernie was not suggesting we transport Marcus all the way down to London! I somehow couldn't picture how a stately funeral procession could be carried out amidst all that heavy traffic along the entirety of the MI and arrive at such a popular venue as Golders Green Crem. on time. It would create havoc with their strictly timed schedule booked for that day and be very upsetting for many other mourners too. It was, to my mind, a most impractical suggestion.

Esther was becoming hysterical by this time and the spoilt poodle was yapping its head off. So Bernie took over and, to smooth things over as best he could, offered me his deepest sympathy, asked if I was all right for money and assured me they would do anything to help, I had only to ask. However, because of Esther's delicate state of health, which he was sure I would understand, they would be unable to undertake the journey from south to north in wintry weather conditions.

I was secretly relieved and quite touched when the largest, and by far the most expensive, floral tribute with a most loving message to Marcus, arrived in due course to accompany him on his farewell journey.

12

Arthur Blenkinsop was in high spirits when, after a brief stop for a quick half-pint of Newcastle Brown at his local, the Braziers' Arms, he and Scruff arrived home at Priory Terrace after their visit to the hospital. On the way home, a new plan of action had been simmering away in Arthur's mind against *them*. Those bloody solicitors – that Mr. Smethers and that Mr. Lybrand. This time, he decided, after what had happened today, both of them were, without the slightest shadow of doubt as guilty as one another.

He could hardly wait to get started on this latest attack of his on them. He could forget about what they had been getting up to with Ethel. As far as he was concerned, that was past history now. Just as well. He wouldn't have time to send any more of his anonymous letters to their offices after this morning anyway. He'd be concentrating his efforts in quite different direction now. Today's events had changed everything entirely.

After fumbling around in all his pockets, he finally managed to locate his front door key. Then, with great concentration, and some difficulty, he inserted the key in the lock.

"Can't see a bloody thing. Black as hell here," he muttered furiously.

He blamed the Council for the poor street lighting. Penny-pinching lot! *They* were the ones to blame for the rising crime rate – muggings and murders and such like violence that went on unchecked these days. Maybe he should write one of his letters to *them* as well. First things first, however. Those lawyers were at the top of his list right now.

"Shuccess at last!" Arthur announced triumphantly as the front door and some of the paintwork thereon, finally yielded to a well-aimed kick and he stepped gingerly over the threshold.

The ever-patient Scruff, followed him hopefully into the pitch dark, unwelcoming house. It was surely high time for some kind of doggie sustenance. Anything would do. Scruff, not having eaten since early that morning, would have been happy to wolf down another helping of those unappetising 'Chummy Chunks', if nothing else was forthcoming. As was the case these days. Ever since the mistress of the house had gone away, meals of any kind had become most irregular.

The house was not the same without Ethel. It had a sick and sour air to it now. Potted plants drooped and wilted for want of water. Furniture had not been dusted or polished for weeks, and floors had not been vacuumed or swept now that Ethel was not there to perform these tasks. The dining room table was covered with newspapers and magazines as well as a stack of unopened post, which Arthur hadn't even glanced at. Why bother? They were in all probability mostly Christmas cards from people they only heard from once a year and the rest were bound to be all bills anyway. That's all people were after these days – money, money, money! Unwashed and unironed clothes lay in forlorn heaps on the bedroom floor, and in the kitchen, supplies of food had not been replenished in the store cupboards. Ethel was the one who had always taken care of all that.

Arthur was feeling hungry. Now that he had switched on the kitchen light, he cast his eyes around him in the vain hope of spotting something easily consumable as a quick snack. He really should have bought fish and chips on the way home, or had a pie and mushy peas with his Newcastle Brown at the pub. His mouth now watered at the mere thought of it. But, he had been anxious to get home as soon as possible to get to work on this latest plan of his.

The kitchen was depressingly devoid of anything in the way of readily consumable food, or even *anything* at all edible for that matter. Everything in the fridge was decidedly 'off', especially that scrawny bird in there, which had turned a very peculiar colour. He'd bought it cheap in the market around Christmas. Why on earth had he done that? He must have been mad! Or maybe he'd intended it as a treat to share with Scruff, which meant he would somehow have had to cook it. But, he told himself, he'd been much too busy for that, what with one thing and another. And now, it certainly smelt as if it was too late. He didn't think he, or even Scruff, would fancy it now.

In the cupboard all that remained now were packets of rice, pasta, oatmeal, flour, sugar, and various other ingredients, which he supposed Ethel would have used for cooking, but he hadn't a clue what to do with them. On the kitchen table were the remains of that 'medicinal' brandy left from this morning and the half-used tin of dog food.

"At least you'll be all right, my bonny lad," Arthur reassured Scruff, putting the last of the Chummy Chunks into Scruff's feeding bowl. He, himself, was feeling a bit dizzy. But then, that was only to be expected – the state his nerves were in, on top of everything else that had happened to him today.

The sooner he got started on that letter the better. But first, he'd put through a phone call to that Mrs. Prettiflower he'd met at the hospital. Poor lass, she'd looked so worried and no wonder. Her husband was just as much a victim of those bloody lawyers as he was. Although, he was bloody well sure that murderous missile had been deliberately thrown from their offices and that it had really been intended for *him* and not Mrs. Prettiflower's husband.

Even so, they, he and Mr. and Mrs. Prettiflower, should work together on making a claim against that lot. He didn't suppose Mr. Prettiflower would be feeling quite up to it yet and, to Arthur's way of thinking, Mrs. Prettiflower looked like the sort of woman who could use his help. She seemed to be not very quick on the uptake. Probably had no idea how to put things in writing. He could tell that by the way she had stared at him when he was explaining things to her at the hospital as if she didn't really understand what he was saying. Oh well, she needn't worry. He had quite a bit of experience of that sort of thing. Letter-writing, that is. Only this time, they would not be anonymous. He'd take care of everything.

With this thought in mind, he poured the last of the brandy into an unwashed glass, which he took from the pile of dirty crockery on the draining board. He manfully swigged down the sickly liqueur with a couple of his pills to calm his nerves. Then he stumbled back to the telephone in the hall to ring the Prettiflower household. It was an easy number to find. It was the only one listed under that name in the telephone directory.

He was staggered by Margot's response. Had she really said '*Dead*'? Maybe he should ring her back and check. Ask her for further information. A few more facts as to what had happened to Mr. Prettiflower and caused him to snuff it would come in useful in pursuing his claim, Arthur told himself. On the other hand, he himself was feeling really queer, sort of sea-sick and his head was going round and round. Later... leave it until later.

These thoughts were abruptly cut short by someone hammering on his front door and persistently flip-flapping the letter-box. Whoever it was, was determined not to be ignored.

Oh shit! He might have guessed! It was that nosey old cow, Ruby Kersley, from Number 9. What did *she* want at this time of night? If she'd come to borrow anything, or wanting to use the telephone, she was out of luck.

"Oh, you are in, then!"

Well that was pretty obvious wasn't it and didn't need any reply from him.

Ruby Kersley's nose was twitching up and down like a rabbit's and she was peering inquisitively past him towards the kitchen. Phew! That smell! What a stink and it looked like a tip in there as far as she could see.

"Ethel, Mrs. Blenkinsop, not back then?"

"No. She's not!"

"Ooh! Gone somewhere warm, has she?"

She was staring pointedly at the hall-stand where Ethel's green winter coat still hung. "Where was it you said she'd gone?"

Bugger the bloody woman! Why did she have to come sticking her nose into his affairs, especially now. And why did her face look like one of those Picasso paintings? All right, he'd tell her about Ethel! Then perhaps she'd leave him in peace. He made a great effort to brace himself and focus on at least one of her fragmented faces.

"If you really, really want to know," he paused, swaying and belching loudly, "she's gone down under, where it's bloody hot and I don't expect to get even an effing post-card from her, where she's gone. Nice of you to ask though," he added, with an attempted sarcastic smile.

Ruby made hurried excuses of having to get back right away 'to see to something cooking in the oven', to justify her hasty departure. Her visit to the Blenkinsop household had confirmed her worst suspicions.

To her way of thinking, that Arthur Blenkinsop was looking downright depraved. She was sure he'd been drinking. And swearing at her like that too! Couldn't look her straight in the eye either. She didn't like the way he'd leered at her when he said Ethel was 'down under'. What did he mean by that? That poor woman, and her such a regular church-goer! She'd often wondered why such a nice young woman as Ethel had married a man like him in the first place.

What had he done to her? There had been no sign of her for some time now. Come to think of it, Ruby hadn't seen her since well before Christmas.

Ruby Kersley was an avid reader of crime novels. Ever since Mr. Kersley had passed away, more years ago than she could remember, reading in bed had been her favourite nightly passion. Not only that, she had read in the newspapers about the dreadful goings-on these days *and* she'd watched all those programmes on the telly about men who committed horrible crimes in cold blood against women. Men who did away with their wives, cut them up and then put them into plastic sacks. Oh my Gawd! Is that what Arthur Blenkinsop had done?

There was that night before Christmas when she'd seen him heaving what could have been a body in one of those outsized black bin-liner into the dust-bin. It could well have been Ethel! If it was, well then, it was her duty to tell *someone* about it, so that proper investigations could be made. And even if it wasn't, Ethel was certainly a missing person, because where was she? *Something* must have happened to her. Who should she tell though?

There was her cousin Mabel's daughter, who had a boyfriend in the police. He'd know what to do about making missing person enquiries. The only trouble was, Ruby herself wasn't on the telephone. Whenever she'd needed to make a phone call in the past, she'd always gone round to Ethel's. Well, of course she couldn't do that now, could she? And she didn't fancy walking round to Mabel's house in the dark. Not these days. It wasn't safe when there were muggers and rapists out there on the prowl, waiting to pounce on their unsuspecting victims, especially innocent little old ladies like herself. But she would go straight round to Mabel first thing in the morning when it was light though. She didn't see why men like Arthur Blenkinsop should get away with murder.

★★★

Arthur closed the door firmly on the fast-retreating Ruby. He had no idea the silly old bitch could move so quickly, with that arthritic hip of hers. He did wonder fleetingly what she was cooking up in her oven, which needed to be rescued so urgently. Nothing was cooking in his own cold and cheerless kitchen, where as far as he could see, most of the cupboards were bare as well. Oh Lord, he could really do with a decent meal right now!

It was moments like this when he found himself missing Ethel. Into his confused mind came snapshot memories of Ethel in those far-off pre-Sharon Hetty Agnes Gertrude days and those brief carefree moments of youthful carnal bliss they had enjoyed together in the stationary cupboard at Bowyers Pharmaceuticals. She was a real goer in those days, tripping provocatively around the office in her high heels and little black mini-skirt.

What a revolution that fashion had caused when it came into existence in the 'sixties. Must have driven many a virile young man mad – not just him. Oh God! The effect it had on him. He could hardly wait for their lunch-time breaks in the stationary cupboard. He could feel an almost forgotten stirring in his loins now at the mere thought of it. Of course, he hastily reminded himself, bringing about an immediate detumescence, Ethel had shown little interest in that direction for ages, at least as far as he was concerned. That was why he was so infuriated when he noticed how she had changed, when she started working for those bloody lawyers.

She'd changed in a number of ways which aroused his suspicions. He'd seen her more than once before she went off to work in the mornings, in front of the hall mirror preening herself, putting make-up on her face – lipstick and stuff – something she hadn't done for years. And, he'd seen her taking slices of her home-made cakes and flowers from the garden too, into the office. She wouldn't be doing all that just for the other typists, he thought darkly. Oh no. It must be for some man or other.

He knew to his cost, all too well what went on in offices, especially in stationary cupboards in stolen moments and he wasn't having any more of that. He'd warned both Smethers and Lybrand in his letters in the strongest possible terms often enough. And then to cap it all, he and Ethel had finally had that flaming row about it.

She had laughed at him. Told him he was a sinner and accused him of other unmentionable things, which he didn't care to dwell on! And said that he should pray for forgiveness for his lustful thoughts. Him! Lustful! Chance would be a fine thing! That really got him so mad that he had hit her. And then…well, that was it really. Now there was just him and Scruff. And it was bloody awful being on his own.

Arthur slumped down at the dining room table. Tears of self-pity welled up in his eyes and he cried like a baby. Then after a few moments, he pushed to one side the pile of unopened mail, and biro in shaky hand, attempted to contrive his latest onslaught on Messrs. Smethers and Lybrand. One way and another, *they* were to blame for all his previous misfortunes – his life was in ruins, his nerves were all to pieces and so were Scruff's and, to cap it all, *someone* in those offices had tried to kill him today.

That nice young doctor, with the tired eyes at the hospital, had nodded his agreement to everything Arthur had told him, even though he hadn't said much except that Arthur ought to go to his own GP, who would know Arthur's case better than anyone, so that he could be referred as a voluntary patient to a specialist in nervous disorders. Arthur had replied that he would be delighted to volunteer to be a patient, having found his present visit so agreeable, especially his handling by the lady para-medics who had brought him there. How was he to know that the young hospital doctor in question had, in fact, been on duty for some twelve hours without a break and could hardly keep his eyes open or stop himself from nodding off from lack of sleep.

Arthur made a supreme, but unsuccessful effort to gather his rambling thoughts together. The biro didn't seem to work and was making jagged scratch marks on the paper. Not only that, household objects in the dining room which were normally never moved only when Ethel dusted them, appeared to be floating and dancing all around him. No, his nerves were certainly in a bad way after this morning. He would need to see his doctor first thing tomorrow, for some more of those pills, which he was now running out of, and to volunteer himself for an appointment with that specialist the hospital doctor had mentioned. Then he'd be more than ready to pursue his claim against Messrs. Smethers and Lybrand.

"Tomorrow," he told himself, lurching his way bedwards, "tomorrow ish another day and it's going to be *the* day of action!"

13

Sandra had not realised how late it was. She had left her charity meeting in good time but had then made a detour into town before returning home. She had been feeling rather guilty over her behaviour towards Charles at breakfast time that morning. She had hardly spoken a word to him, ignoring his pleas for sympathy over what was clearly just a hang-over. For one who was usually so moderate in all things, he had somewhat surprisingly rather over-indulged as regards cheese and wine the night before, thus failing to fulfil her expectations. She had been so annoyed she sent him off to the office without even a wifely peck on the cheek and the silly old darling had looked quite put out when he left the house this morning.

She decided she would make up for her coolness towards him by preparing a really romantic supper this evening accompanied by a bottle of that wine he'd so obviously enjoyed last night. She had, therefore, gone out of her way to call in at that special butcher's shop in town, renowned throughout the area for the quality of their prime cuts of beef. Charles liked his steak rather rare. And tonight, she would cook it just the way he liked it. Then, there were candles and perfume to be bought and there was a spur of the moment visit to that new lingerie boutique where there just happened to be a black lace negligee, which to Sandra's mind, would be just right for what she had planned as a finale to the perfect evening. Finally, rather later than intended, a visit to the wine merchant for the wine.

A cluster of customers, who appeared to be in no great hurry to leave the premises, were engrossed with the sales assistant in some ghoulish gossipy chit-chat of which Sandra only caught snatches, as she politely, but firmly forced her way to the counter.

"It was some kind of flying object what hit him. So they said. In the Passage…"

"Naw! Git away! I don't believe in them UFOs. D'you?"

"Well, what else could it have been then? You tell me…"

"Terrorist attack, d'you think?"

"Could've been. Never know these days, with all them foreigners around…"

"Do excuse me, won't you?" Sandra bestowed her most dazzling smile all round. "So sorry but I must get home to my children. Do you mind? I only want just the one bottle of the Shiraz, please."

The shop assistant served her absentmindedly, reluctant to miss further details of the disaster currently under discussion. Then, presumably out of courtesy for this most recent customer, turning to Sandra, she informed her,

"Eh, you'd never credit the things that go on in this place, would you? In broad daylight too. I mean a terrible accident like that…"

"No, no! You most certainly wouldn't," agreed Sandra, with another of her dazzling smiles. She hurriedly paid for her purchase and dashed out of the shop.

She'd no idea what they were talking about and was quite sure it was of no possible interest to her anyway.

"Ghouls," she thought sourly, "they'd no doubt flock to see a public hanging, if they still existed!"

No need to though these days, when there was such a wealth

of death and destruction to be viewed on TV from the comfort of their own sofas and armchairs.

With any luck, she'd be home before Charles. Monique would have made sure the children were all bathed and ready for bed. Oh Christ! She had just remembered she'd promised Monique she wouldn't be late so that Monique could meet up with friends in town that evening. Firmly pressing down on the accelerator, she headed for home at top speed.

As she turned into the drive, Sandra could see in her headlights a ramshackle car parked outside the partially open front door. And there was Monique, standing there in her disco flimsy finery, her dangling ear-rings sparkling in the hallway light, all ready to dash off with her friends the moment Sandra arrived.

★★★

Earlier that evening, Monique had been looking forward to her evening in town. Her friend, Marianne, and her boyfriend had promised to give her a lift. The Hardy children had been successfully bribed with extra sweets and chocolates into agreeing to an earlier-than-usual bedtime.

So, with them safely stowed away in their beds with whatever comics or books they themselves had decided upon, however unsuitable, Monique was making her own early preparations for the evening. She was enjoying a long, lazy soak in a bath, to which she'd added a liberal amount of Sandra's most expensive and much advertised bath oil, guaranteed to enhance feminine allure. She was also planning to help herself to Sandra's Christian Dior perfume after her bath, when suddenly she thought she heard the doorbell ring.

"Merde!" Monique had not expected Sandra to be home quite so early nor to be caught out making liberal use of Sandra's cosmetics. Why was she ringing the doorbell, instead of letting herself in with her own key? How inconsiderate of her, especially at a time like this! Although, maybe it wasn't Sandra, in which case, whoever it was would either ring again, or go away.

The doorbell rang again. No wonder she hadn't quite heard it before. Whoever it was must have rung the bell in a 'sorry-to-disturb-you' sort of way. Which meant it certainly wasn't Sandra! Maybe her friend, Marianne, had arrived early – much too early, thought Monique, not giving her time to get ready properly. Surely *all* French girls, not just Parisians, should know such matters as preparing for a date, blind or otherwise, took time and careful preparation!

Monique having hurriedly pulled out the bath plug, just in case it was Sandra waiting to be let in, grabbed up her bath robe and dashed downstairs.

A pale, exhausted woman, clutching a large bunch of funereal lilies, stood on the doorstep. "F…for poor Mrs. Hardy," she stammered, somewhat taken aback by being confronted by the spectacle of Monique in a state of undress. At the same time, relieved that it wasn't poor Mrs. Hardy herself.

"Yes, yes. She is out now. I give it to her. Thank you very much," Monique replied curtly, quickly closing the front door against the cold blast of air and wondering why anyone should refer to her well-to-do employer as 'poor'.

She assumed the flowers had been ordered by Mr. Hardy to make up for not being home tonight. Or perhaps it was to mark some kind of anniversary. What a strange choice of bouquet! But then, Mr. Hardy was English and lacked the savoir-faire of Frenchmen, who would have chosen red roses for their wives and mistresses. Certainly not something which looked as if it was meant to be placed upon a coffin! she told herself, as she carried the flowers disdainfully through to the kitchen and put them in the centre of the table where Sandra would be sure to see them as soon as she came in.

Monique dashed off back upstairs. She had other more important things to think about, like getting herself ready for her evening out.

★★★

"I'm so sorry, Monique! The traffic was simply ghastly and..."

The rest of Sandra's sentence was drowned out by a sharp 'parp-parp' on the car horn of the old banger waiting on the drive. Monique's friends felt they had waited quite long enough. The engine was running. The rear passenger door had been swung open ready to receive Monique as she teetered across the icy surface of the drive in her precariously high heels.

Dismissing Sandra's apologies with a magnanimous wave of her hand, as she dived into the fuggy interior of the car, Monique called out her assurance that the children were all in bed and fast asleep now, and that there was a written message and some flowers for Sandra in the kitchen. Then, in a cloud of exhaust fumes, she and her friends were gone.

"Selfish little bitch!" thought Sandra. "Dashing off like that!"

Then she reminded herself that when she was Monique's age an evening of loud music, flashing disco lights and gyrating on a pin-head of a dance-floor would have been her idea of unmissable fun, too. Monique was, after all, good with the children. Someone she could trust and rely on.

So, having quickly checked that the children were, in fact, all safely tucked up and fast asleep in bed, Sandra was able to relax. She was in no doubt that she and Charles would be able to enjoy some quality time together this evening.

How fortunate it was that Charles was not yet home. He was so conscientious he was probably working late in the office. That's what Monique must have meant when she said there was a message for Sandra, by the telephone in the kitchen. So, she calculated, this would give her ample time to make preparations for their romantic evening, dining by candlelight.

She'd make sure that everything was just perfect. She would set the table in the dining room with their best cutlery and crystal glasses, usually reserved for very special occasions. Flowers. She needed flowers as a centre-piece for the table to complete her perfect arrangement. Dammit! She'd forgotten to buy any flowers. Hold it, though, Monique had mentioned something about a delivery of flowers. They must be from Charles. He was sure to have chosen something which would be just perfect for this romantic evening, the darling man.

As she entered the kitchen, the cloying scent of the lilies assailed her nostrils. And Sandra stared in disbelief at the bouquet of white lilies tied with purple satin ribbon, on the table. Not at all what she expected. These were obviously not from Charles. But who on earth could have sent them to her? It must have been a misdelivery. That was the obvious answer. But no. There was an envelope attached to the bouquet with her name on it in bold black letters. How very odd. There was probably a card inside with a message and name of sender.

It was then that she spotted the note Monique had left for her on the kitchen dresser and she was dumbfounded by it. What the hell did Charles mean by saying he 'wouldn't be home *at all*'?

She was aware that he had seemed rather put out when he left that morning. Well, to be truthful, she had been rather a bitch to him. And the children too, had been particularly irritating, in the absence of Monique. But surely he couldn't have taken it so much to heart, could he? Oh God! Had she really hurt him that much?

Maybe there was something else preying on his mind. Something at the office, perhaps which would explain why he wouldn't be home until very late. She remembered that he had mentioned something about a series of anonymous letters he'd been getting from some nutter. She thought at the time when he told her about it that he hadn't really seemed too put out over it. No, it couldn't have been anything to do with that, she concluded. So what was it that was troubling him?

The note said quite clearly that he wouldn't be home 'at all' and Charles was quite meticulous in his choice of words. Sandra tried to recall what she had said which might have upset him so deeply. Nothing. Just the opposite, in fact. She hadn't said *anything*. He must have read much more into that stubborn silence of hers than was intended.

Like every other couple, they had had their fair share of rows now and again, But they'd always made up their differences quite quickly, until now. To Sandra's way of thinking, making up after their quarrels played an important part in strengthening their marriage. She had made sure of that. And she had fully intended to do so tonight. But the tone of this message suggested she had somehow managed to hurt him more deeply than usual.

Well, she'd soon put that right! He was probably still in the office. Burying himself in his work, the silly, stubborn darling. She'd ring him now and persuade him to come home right away. She dialled the office number but there was no reply, other than the recorded message informing callers that the offices of Smethers & Lybrand were now closed but to call again during normal office hours from 8.30a.m to 5.30 p.m. She put the receiver down, wondering where he could be and what she should do next.

Charles was not the sort of man to go off drinking in pubs or wine-bars. Maybe he'd calmed down after sending her that curt message and was already on his way home. If so, then she'd better get on with her plans for their romantic evening.

First she must clear this extraordinary bouquet away from her work surface. And that reminded her, there was that envelope which she hadn't opened yet, attached to the flowers. Maybe she should look to see who had sent her this unusual bouquet.

On a black-edged card which she drew out from the envelope, in flowing Gothic letters of gold, were inscribed the words:

'Deepest sympathy in your sad and sudden loss of
a dear and loving husband.
Today on Earth – tomorrow in the heavenly
kingdom of Our Lord.'

The florist had taken considerable trouble over the selection of this card. She thought these words singularly appropriate in the unfortunate circumstances.

Sandra, on the other hand, was as bemused and confused by that message as by the other one from Charles. She didn't know whether to laugh or cry. Was this someone's idea of a sick joke? It was in very bad taste if it was. Could Charles himself have sent it? No. Not his style at all! Besides, whenever Charles sent her flowers they were usually something exotic and expensive, like orchids or red roses, which he knew she adored.

A scrap of soggy, crumpled paper had fallen out from the laurel leaves which formed a background to the lilies. She sat down on one of the kitchen stools, absentmindedly smoothing out the scrap of paper. Something had obviously been hastily scrawled in capitals on one of Messrs. Smethers and Lybrand's distinctive memo pads. Who, from that office, other than Charles himself would be sending her flowers and with such a bizarre message too? Maybe this would help to solve the mystery.

With careful scrutiny, Sandra could just make out the words:

'SEND FLOWERS TO MRS. HARDY' and 'ACCIDENT VICTIM'.

She read this several times with increasing bewilderment. Then, quite suddenly she recalled the snatches of overheard conversation in the wine-merchants about some fatality which had happened close by there, that very afternoon. Sandra now wished she had paid more attention.

"A man," one of the ghouls had said, "had been struck down by…" some unlikely object, or other…"in the Passage."

"…*in the Passage*…" Well, that must have been Friargate Passage, where Charles's offices were.

At the time she had assumed the speaker was referring to part of the victim's anatomy.

Oh God! Could it have been Charles who was…? Oh dear God, no! Then had he had some kind of premonition? Hence his message about 'not coming home at all'?

If so, then was Charles, her dearest, darling Charles…? Sandra whispered the word "*dead*"? And was the bouquet of lilies someone's clumsy idea of breaking the news gently and urgently to her? Not realising that Sandra would not be at home.

Maybe that super-efficient temp that Charles had mentioned once or twice had arranged for the flowers to be sent, or brought them to the house herself, Or that none-too-bright office junior, who according to Charles, had exasperated him on several occasions, perhaps she been asked to deliver them. If not, who else could it have been?

If only Monique had not rushed off in such a hurry, Sandra could have asked her. But, enough of these meandering thoughts. It didn't matter who'd sent the flowers or who had brought them. More importantly, what had happened to Charles and where was he now? She must pull herself together and think things through rationally.

If something really awful had happened to Charles and she still couldn't quite believe this to be so, then she must find out for certain. There was no point in ringing the office. There was no one there now, as she had already found out. Then who else should she ring? Police? Hospital?

She decided to ring the hospital first. Maybe Charles had only been injured. Of course! He couldn't die and leave her just like that! Not when she'd had everything planned out for this evening. No. If he had been the accident victim mentioned at the wine merchants then he must have been taken to the hospital after the 'accident'. She decided to ring there right away. She searched through the telephone directory for the number of the General Hospital.

It was as Sandra picked up the telephone receiver and started to dial the hospital number, that Charles walked in. Overwhelmed with relief, she dropped the phone and rushed over to him. He looked grey and drawn, but brightened somewhat as Sandra flung her arms round him. She hugged him tightly to her, crying,

"Oh Charles, my darling! Oh my love. You're here. You're home!"

The darling girl! How loving and understanding she was. He had not expected such a touching show of affection on his return. It helped to ease the distress of the news he, himself, had so recently received after making enquiries at the hospital as to the welfare of the accident victim.

"Yes, I'm home," he smiled wearily, "but I'm afraid I've some rather bad news to tell you."

"Bad news?"

How could it be bad news when he was home, safe and sound?

"It can't be all that terrible, can it? I'm sure you'll be able to deal with it darling. Just tell me what it is and…"

"I'm afraid," he replied slowly, " Smethers and Lybrand are going to be in big trouble and it's probably all my fault. I think I may have killed a man today."

14

That fateful day when Marcus had been so tragically struck down, both Charles and Sandra Hardy had each in their own way received a terrible shock. Sandra clung fiercely to her bewildered husband, as if she would never let him go. Her body pressed against him, she stroked his hair and whispered words of comfort over and over again.

Charles was overwhelmed by her tender concern for him. How wonderful she was! Sandra was his tower of strength. She would help him to get through this nightmare situation now facing him. He felt he had never needed her so much as at that moment. He'd tell her everything. He'd start by telling her all about that accursed cheese.

"Sandra, darling, I have to tell you…" he began.

"Ssh! Not now. Whatever it is, my darling love, can wait. We'll talk about it later, much later…" she murmured.

He was here. Thank God! He was alive after all.

She wanted him so much. Her need was strong and physical. She was swamped by an urgent desire for him to make love to her. She could feel his body too, responding to hers. He was kissing her long and hard. There was no need for words. Then, hand in hand, leaving the cloying scent of the funereal lilies and the unopened bottle of wine behind them, they went slowly upstairs to their bedroom.

That night, their love-making was the most passionate they had experienced for a very long time. Then, as they lay side by side in sweet, exhausted content, they discussed in low whispers, so as not to wake the children, the events of that most extraordinary day and began to make plans for dealing with any possible outcome arising from that day's tragic accident.

★★★

"But darling, you can't possibly blame yourself for what happened to that poor man!"

"Yes, but…I chucked that damn cheese out onto the balcony and…"

"And how do you know that cheese had anything to do with the accident? What proof is there?"

"Well,…all I know is…"

"Charles, darling, for all you know it could have been caused by something else. You didn't actually see what happened, did you?"

"Well no. But my darling girl, what else could it have been?"

"Oh, lots of other things. There are always repairs going on around your offices aren't there, on those old buildings? That's why builders wear those special yellow helmets. There might be bits of masonry and timber falling down at any time on someone or something. It does happen, you know."

Then remembering the conversation she had overheard at the wine merchants, "In fact, in this space age of ours it could have been *anything* falling from above, couldn't it? Not just from your building, but from out of the blue. Let's say it could have been 'an unidentified object from an unknown source'."

Although Charles did not reply, he was clearly turning this idea over in his mind. Sandra certainly possessed a more imaginative turn of mind than he did. In spite of not having actually taken her final exams, her time as a law student had not been entirely wasted and, being somewhat of a born advocate, she eventually lead her troubled and exhausted husband round to accepting her view of the tragic event that on the balance of probabilities and without any evidence to the contrary, the whole question of liability in relation to that unfortunate cheese was highly questionable. Finally Sandra said,

"Besides, there weren't any witnesses were there? Anyone offering to make a statement?"

Charles considered her question carefully before replying,

"No—o. At least, not as far as I know."

"And was anyone else injured by this 'falling object'? Anyone else needing hospital treatment?"

"Well, there was some queer fellow and his dog…"

"*A dog?*"

"Yes. Darling, please don't interrupt. Let me finish. I was given to understand quite unofficially, of course, that he insisted on being seen by one of the medics in Casualty, who thought he was a bit of a nutter and referred him for psychiatric assessment."

Sandra was relieved.

"Oh then we needn't worry about him then, need we? But I think you should have a word with old MacAndrew as soon as possible, darling. Don't you agree?"

"Yes, yes!" Charles replied wearily. "I'll see to it first thing tomorrow."

Alan MacAndrew was the ancient local coroner. He played an irregular game of golf with Charles and was a frequent dinner party guest at their home. Even at his age, he still had an eye for a pretty woman and he considered Charles to be a hell of a lucky fellow to have a ravishing red-head with such gorgeous legs as had Sandra. Alan MacAndrew was fast approaching what he hoped would be a blissfully trouble-free retirement. At this stage in his life, he was far from inclined to make decisions that, in his considered opinion, would lead to unnecessarily protracted discussions and investigations.

"Well then darling, in the circumstances, he'll almost certainly regard this as just another death by misadventure, won't he?"

"Umm." Charles fervently hoped so as he drifted off into a far from untroubled sleep.

15

The following morning, the secretaries' office at Smethers and Lybrand was a-buzz with speculation.

"They're *all* in there. The whole lot of them. I wonder what it's all about. Must be something important. They all look dead serious. They've asked me to make coffee for them," Carol announced breathlessly.

She'd just returned from the board room where an *ad hoc* partners' meeting was already in progress.

"Did you hear anything of what they were saying?"

"Is it about that accident, yesterday? D'you think that cheese had anything to do with it?"

"Did they say anything about that? It doesn't seem to be out there on the balcony any more."

"Don't be daft! How could it have been the cheese?"

"Yes but *if* it was that cheese, then what do you think is going to happen now? And have they said who was to blame?"

Carol looked somewhat crestfallen. It was flattering to be the centre of attention for once in this office, where as the office junior, her views on anything really important were usually disregarded. But she couldn't really answer any of these questions. So what could she actually tell them, unless she made something up?

"I don't know," she admitted reluctantly. "They stopped talking when I was in the room, except to ask me to make the coffee," she added brightly. "Mr. Hardy particularly asked for black coffee."

"Then you'd better get on with it, hadn't you," suggested Amy, lips pursed.

Much though she would have liked to continue taking part in the fascinating subject under discussion by the other secretaries of yesterday's unfortunate events, the burning question as to what had actually happened to the cheese and where it was now, she had mountains of work to deal with and, no doubt, there would now be a confidential report for her to word process, as an outcome of this morning's partners' meeting. She'd be the one working late yet again this evening since the Busy Bees Agency had not so far found a replacement for Ethel, Mr. Hardy's temp.

It was in fact nearly lunch-time when Amy was summoned to Charles Hardy's office. Glancing up at her with a faintly puzzled expression from the sheaf of papers spread over his desk, as she entered the room, he said,

"Ethel, still not back then? Ah well Amy, I'm sure we can leave all this in your capable hands."

Amy's heart sank, as several sheets of Charles's indecipherably scrawled notes were passed across to her. It would take her a hell of a time to puzzle her way through them, she thought ruefully. She'd be working through her lunch break today, that was for sure. And, probably working late as well. It was times like this when, although she had never really taken to Ethel, that she missed her and fervently wished Ethel was still there.

"Copies to go to all the partners and one on file, of course. No need to tell you I'm sure that all this is strictly confidential," Charles reminded her with an encouraging smile.

Last night, he had felt completely shattered. But after talking everything through with Sandra and after having made an early morning call to old MacAndrew, matters appeared to be far less bleak. In fact, he was feeling surprisingly cheerful this morning when he arrived at the office and was rather pleased with himself for the way in which he had taken control of the *ad hoc* meeting he had called for at an unusually early hour of the day.

He had observed with some degree of grim amusement the various expressions on the faces of his colleagues as they drifted into the boardroom and took their seats around the table. Some had evidently had a heavy night judging from their somewhat hung-over appearance, others looked slightly apprehensive as to the purpose of this early morning meeting, and were probably wondering if some difficult client of theirs was making a serious complaint specifically against *them* about something they had, or had not done.

As soon as Charles was satisfied that all his fellow partners were present, he sent an urgent message through to the secretaries' office for coffee, which appeared to be strongly indicated. Then he launched straight into the main topic for discussion, under the heading of : 'Accident in close proximity to the premises of Lybrand & Smethers on the 10th January.'

Only one of the other partners, Piers Robinson, newly recruited to their Litigation Department, and over-brimming with youthful enthusiasm and self-importance at his shining new status, admitted to being aware that there had been an occurrence of this nature. The others listened in inscrutable silence as Charles gave a brief, carefully rehearsed account of the fatality. Sandra, the dear girl, had stayed up half the night drafting and redrafting this for him. She was one in a million! What would he have done without her? He would have to think of some special way of showing her his appreciation. But back to more immediate matters.

"To sum up therefore," Charles concluded, "this tragic incident, which unfortunately occurred in the close proximity to our premises, resulted from an unidentified falling object from an unknown source."

Having reached the end of his prepared statement, he paused, sat back with affected ease and, glancing round the room, tried to gauge the reaction from his colleagues.

Piers Robinson was the first to comment.

"There's no mention of that stinking cheese in your report, is there, Charles?" he drawled, with what Charles regarded as unwarranted over-familiarity. "I was wondering if that could possibly have had anything to do with it, since I'd heard a rumour that certain steps had been taken to rid the house of Smethers and Lybrand of that plaguey cheese by casting it forth into the Great Beyond."

What *was* the impudent puppy talking about? Puzzled looks were exchanged between some of the others round the table especially by those who had been out of the office that particular morning or who had been completely unaware of the existence of that unfortunate object.

"*Cheese*? How could anyone be killed by *cheese*! Love the stuff myself. You can't beat a good Stilton with a glass of port."

"What's cheese got to do with some chap or other being fatally injured outside our offices, for Christ's sake? Dashed bad luck but not our concern. Surely?"

"Doesn't it raise the question of liability?" persisted Piers. "I mean if it was that cheese...the one that was in our offices..."

"Ah yes! Good point, Piers." Charles was more than ready for this bumptious young puppy after Sandra's thorough briefing. "*If*, as you so rightly say, it was the cheese, or indeed any other cheese, that struck the fatal blow, what evidence is there to prove this? And, from what I understand, the actual object has not been identified. It could, therefore, have been any falling object which caused the unfortunate accident. We do not know. Don't you agree?"

He glanced around the table for confirmation on this point.

There were murmurs of assent from those who felt they had more important matters awaiting their attention in their own offices than to waste any more of their valuable time, but Piers Robinson was not to be so easily put off.

"Perhaps you could tell us what happened to the cheese. The one you put out on the balcony, Charles?"

"Regrettably no," replied Charles, loftily. "There is no trace of it. None whatsoever. More than likely it was snapped up by some light-fingered element, which one does observe loitering around in these parts from time to time. And," he added for good measure, "I understand there were no reliable witnesses to the actual occurrence."

He fervently hoped that this was indeed so.

"Then I hardly think it need concern us," wheezed old Matthew Trotter testily, rising shakily to his feet. "And we should now bring this meeting to a close."

The old boy was in urgent need of the 'Gents' after two cups of coffee, which always had an immediate diuretic effect on him.

Charles looked up from the notes he had been making during the morning's discussion, and nodded his agreement with old Trotter's timely suggestion.

"Thank you, all of you, for giving up your time this morning. I'll make sure you all have a copy of my report and have a copy placed on file for reference, in the unlikely event of there being any further discussion arising from this incident at some future date."

"Oh, and just one final point," he added, remembering Sandra's practical advice about the disposal of that fancy bouquet of funeral lilies, "as this tragedy occurred on our doorstep, so to speak, I take it you all agree that in the circumstances, it would be a suitable gesture from a firm of our reputation and high standing in the local community, to show our concern by sending some appropriate floral tribute to the victim's widow, a Mrs. Prettiflower. Agreed?"

16

When I woke on that funeral morning, the snow, which had begun to fall the night before, was still falling in tiny angel feather flakes, covering the garden with a magical carpet of soft shimmering whiteness. The only marks to be seen were the patterns left by birds searching for food and the footprints of a hungry scavenging fox. The trees, which Marcus loved so much, were garlanded in silver splendour, against the cold clear sky.

I heard Cathy calling to me. She was already up and was busy in the kitchen making porridge for our breakfast. Shortly after her arrival to stay with me, she had cleared my larder and refrigerator of all high cholesterol items, in fact all the foods Marcus enjoyed eating, replacing them with what she described as 'healthy options'. She had insisted that this was part of the 'Margot make-over plan', which had included a stylish haircut, new make-up and a new black and white outfit for me, to be worn for the funeral with the pearl necklace and ear-rings Marcus had given me for our last anniversary.

Looking at my reflection in the hall mirror before setting out for the crematorium that morning, I hardly recognised the unfamiliar image which stared back at me. I turned to Cathy for reassurance.

"How do I look? You don't think it's…it's too…?"

"If it's the new hair colour you're worried about, it's just right for the new 'you', duckie. A widow can go gold with grief, according to Oscar Wilde, didn't you know? You look great. Honestly. Marcus would have loved it," she reassured me.

Yes, I suppose he would. My hair was now the colour of mature double Gloucester. All the same, I decided to cover my head with the wide-brimmed black hat I had worn for my mother's funeral a few years back. It would serve to hide any tears that I couldn't control.

Mother would have approved of my decision about the hat. According to her early teaching on good manners, based upon her diligent study of the behaviour of the royal family, whom she worshipped, although she had never actually been within curtseying distance of any of them, there were certain things one must *never* do in public. 'Eating in the streets' was one of these aberrations, she impressed upon me when I was a child. Well, you simply couldn't imagine any one of those well-behaved royals sauntering along sucking a bull's-eye or a gob-stopper, when they were doing a walk-about, now could you?

And then, as I grew up, she impressed upon me that it was of paramount importance that one's emotions should *never* be shown in public. Crying, kissing and cuddling, especially if it involved members of the opposite sex, were strictly private acts.

"You never see any of the royal family doing it, do you?" Mother maintained.

There was no answer to that one. Although it led Cathy and me to speculate in secrecy as to when and where *they* did do it, especially Victoria and Albert, who had produced all those nine children without ever having been observed to embrace, or even hold hands, in public. Fortunately, for the sake of Mother's peace of mind, she did not live to witness that much publicised balcony kiss between Charles and Diana in the summer of 1981.

At Mother's funeral I had been puzzled by Marcus's unexpected tears, as the prayer by St. Francis 'Oh Lord, make me an instrument of thy peace…' was being said, followed by William Blake's *'Divine Image'*: 'To Mercy, Pity Peace and Love /All pray in their distress,/And to these virtues of delight,/ Return their thankfulness.'

I reached across and took his hand in mine so that we could comfort one another. I hadn't realised that he felt so deeply for her, or had he? Theirs had been a kind of uneasy truce. It was later that day, as we drove away after Mother's funeral, that Marcus explained. It had been for him at last, an opportunity in this formal setting, to give expression to his feelings for the loss of his own beloved parents. He never knew exactly when or how his parents met their end. Then I realised how hard it must have been for him to carry this sense of loss deep inside him all this time, and our shared sorrow brought us even closer together.

It had not been easy for Mother to accept Marcus's foreign origins, when he and I first met. Although, as far as I was concerned, this was all part of his irresistible charm.

"*Where* did you say he was from?"

"From Germany, Mother, but he…'

"Oh Margot! We were at war with Germany! Have you forgotten? Your grandfather and your father were killed by the Germans."

"But Mother, he didn't chose to be born in that country any more than you or I chose to be born here. Besides, Marcus fought for this country. And he's British now!"

I decided not to mention Marcus's Jewish origins to her at that time. It would have been too much for her, with her narrow outlook and inherent prejudices, to bear. Poor Mother, she was obviously distressed enough by the thought of her daughter even going out with someone whom she still regarded as 'the enemy' although the war had been over for some fourteen years when I met Marcus in the late 1950s.

As for her asking me if I had forgotten about my grandfather and my father, well, I had never really known either of them! My grandfather had died long before I was born and, as for my father, he was killed early on in WW2, when I was just two years old. All I ever knew of him was that photograph in the silver frame on Mother's dressing table. It was of a fair-haired young man in air force officer's uniform. He looked so young. Just a boy really. How could he possibly be *my father*? Sadly, I had no memory of him as an actual physical presence.

"And I don't know what your grandmother would have said about it," she persisted for good measure.

My memories of my grandmother were of a tight-lipped old lady, who appeared to disapprove of almost everything and everyone. She always wore black, as if she were in perpetual mourning throughout her life. She hardly ever stirred from the armchair by the fireside in winter and in summer. As she belonged to the local church's Sewing Circle, she was for ever knitting babies bootees, bed-socks, tea-cosies and egg-cosies for the church bazaars. Occasionally a group of her cronies, other members of the Sewing Circle, would arrive at our house to take afternoon tea with her. Over the click-clack of their knitting-needles and the chinking of tea-cups, they would commiserate over the shocking state the world was now in. Inevitably, they came to the same conclusion. What was the world coming to? It was all down to the deterioration of moral standards since their young days. And the outrageous behaviour of 'the working classes' and the Labour movement, to which none of them, quite definitely belonged. So I could well imagine that Grandmother would not have had anything positive to say about my introducing a *foreigner* into the household.

Mother, having been widowed so young, had focused her attention fiercely and protectively on me, her one and only child. In spite of her earlier misgivings as to Marcus's unBritish origins, she was clearly pleased that I was to become engaged and then married at nineteen. So much younger than the daughters of her circle of acquaintances, thus making her the object of their secret envy. Unmarried daughters, those 'left on the shelf' in their late twenties, were a source of embarrassment to their mothers. Marriage and white weddings were still very much in vogue in those pre-bra-burning, pre-pill, pre-feminine emancipation days. No self-respecting mother wanted to see *her* daughter 'left on the shelf' to become an old maid, or suffer an even worse fate by becoming pregnant before the church bells had metaphorically been rung for the wedding.

There was, however, another shock in store for Mother, when I told her of our plans.

"A *Registry Office* wedding! And so soon too. Hardly any time for me to make proper arrangements. I had always hoped to see you walking down the aisle at St. Michael's. Oh Margot! Why a *Registry Office*? You're not...are you?"

Of course I wasn't! Pregnant, I mean. Marcus was an honourable man, adhering to the moral mores of his own upbringing. But for my mother, even though neither she, nor I, were regular churchgoers, a Registry Office wedding in those days could only mean 'one thing'.

It was because of my own religious uncertainties at that time and because, of course, Marcus was certainly not C of E. Although he had turned his back on the country of his birth, and made great efforts to unlearn much which had formed part of his early upbringing, out of respect for his parents and his forefathers, he could not renounce his ethnic identity. He was, if anything, a secular Jew. But, as he was eager for us to marry as soon as possible, once I'd said 'yes' to his proposal, he and I agreed it should be a civil marriage ceremony.

I'm not sure even now that Mother fully understood the real reasons for our choice of a civil wedding. Even when I tried to explain to her about Marcus's background, I don't think she was able to appreciate the contribution that he and other refugees like him, lawyers, doctors, scientists, musicians, had made to our country and that we would have been poorer economically and culturally without them.

Oddly enough, Mother did not object to Marcus on the grounds that he was older than me. He was, after all, she proudly proclaimed to her friends, a Professor of Languages. Which was not strictly true. As well as carrying out his full-time occupation in the import-export business, Marcus was teaching evening classes in German at the college where I was taking a secretarial course. He had an extraordinary capacity for working long hours and studying tremendously hard. Initially, it was for him a matter of sheer survival in a country where he, had no family to support him financially. And later, after gaining an external university degree, he was determined to demonstrate his gratitude to his adopted country by becoming as independent and successful as possible in whatever employment he was able to secure.

He was equally determined in his decision to marry me, from the first moment we had shared the same table in the College canteen. As Fate would have it, I'd made a spur of the moment decision to have a cup of coffee in the canteen before going home one summer evening. I was amazed that he, this marvellous man with brown smiling eyes and just the hint of an accent in that deep velvety voice of his, should show interest in me and then invite me to my first-ever attendance at Covent Garden to a performance of Wagner's *Lohengrin*! I was no golden Rhinemaiden – just a little suburban brown mouse! Throughout our years together, Marcus taught me so much about music and extended my knowledge of composers beyond the boundaries of the United Kingdom.

And now that he's gone, I count myself as having been blessed by good fortune in those years Marcus and I were able to share our joys and our sorrows. True to one another and forsaking all others. Unlike Cathy. I'd lost count of her numerous partners. It has always been a mystery to me how her love-life was such a muddle when she was so good at organising other things, especially for other people. It was that part of our friendship I most valued.

I can't imagine how I would have managed without her help at the time of Marcus's fatal accident. There was so much to be done. We can't just shuffle off our mortal coils in our civilised society. Apart from all the arrangements for the funeral and a celebration of Marcus's life to follow, there were the masses of paper-work to be attended to.

The funeral had, so Cathy assured me after the event, gone off very smoothly. Apart that is, from the unexpected appearance of an uninvited guest, of which I will tell you more in detail later.

My own recollection of the actual funeral service was rather hazy, highlighted with tear-soaked tissues and pin-points of pain. A broken heart does not repair instantly. The pain lingers on until one is able to finally accept that pain and sorrow are a vital part of our human existence, from which we finally emerge with new-born strength and understanding if we make the effort to do so.

17

It had stopped snowing by the time we came out of the crematorium chapel to the last lingering notes of Mozart's *Requiem*. It was treacherously icy underfoot and still freezing cold, although a feeble wintry sun was trying to shine.

There was a bewildering crowd of people gathered outside the building, most of them so well muffled against the cold it was difficult to distinguish individual features. Who were they all? In my benumbed state of grief, I couldn't seem to recognise anyone. I supposed most of them were former business colleagues and associates and their wives. Or maybe not. Maybe they were there for the service just before, or the one just after Marcus's. Crematoriums work to a very tight time-schedule.

I found myself wondering how many mourners end up attending the wrong funeral. Even in the most efficient conveyor-belt system for dealing with the dispatching of our loved ones to the Great Unknown, I suppose it *could* happen. Heaven forbid! Although, according to Cathy, and she should know, there are some old ladies who are compulsive funeral-goers. They regularly trot along to any funeral they can find that happens to be taking place in their neighbourhood, without any connection whatsoever with the deceased. I wonder if this could possibly be as a kind of dress rehearsal for their own departure from this Earth. Or perhaps it's an economical way of feeding themselves by joining in the various wakes after the funeral services.

If anything, there appeared to be an even bigger crowd later at the 'Celebration of Life' for Marcus, at the Eastledale Country Hotel, where refreshments were being served. I was somewhat worried that Cathy had gone over the top in the sending out of invitations to attend this 'Celebration of Life' after the funeral. Or it could have been that the Athlone Suite, the room in which the 'Celebration' was held, was normally used for business conferences of one kind or another. So perhaps some of those who were participating so enthusiastically in the 'Celebration', were under the impression this was all part of their training programme that day. Anyway, Marcus would have been pleased to see such a good turn-out, with so many people enjoying themselves.

Cathy had assured me she had good reasons for this particular choice of venue.

"It will be so much easier for you if everyone goes there after the service rather than coming back here to the house," Cathy had explained when she was making these arrangements. "That way, you'll be able to slip away quietly whilst they're all eating and drinking and no one will notice that you've gone. Believe me duckie, it'll be much better for you at a time like this to get away as soon as you can, put your feet up and shed a few tears if you want to, in the privacy and comfort of your own home."

She was right, of course. I was feeling really low and more than ready to leave the 'Celebration', after the ordeal of receiving so many murmured condolences, vague offers to 'let us know if we can do anything', plus a very tempting offer to make use of a holiday apartment in Majorca to 'get away from it all' whenever I felt I needed to do so.

This offer came from someone called Justin Walker, who introduced himself to me as an ex-colleague of Marcus. He was tall and rather distinguished-looking in a very olde-English sort of way and I caught a whiff of expensive after-shave as he came close to me. I couldn't really remember much about him, other than Marcus had once referred to him as 'a bit of a ladies' man', with a string of ex-wives and girlfriends to prove it. Pressing one of his business cards into my hand, and gazing deep into my eyes, he confided that he had left 'the old firm' and was now running his own computer business.

"Do get in touch with me whenever you need me," he murmured. "I'll be more than ready and willing to help at any time."

I had noticed him earlier having an animated conversation with Cathy, who from the sparkle in her eye, could well have been weighing up adding another Mr. Right or Wrong to her list.

From the babble of voices and the clinking of glasses, it certainly sounded as if everyone else there, whoever they were, was having a very jolly time. Marcus, excellent party host that he was, would have approved. It was, after all, in celebration of *his* life they had gathered together.

I was about to make a discreet exit when I spotted *him* and his dog. That weird man from the hospital. He, and his dog, both looked as if they had had too much to drink. He was clutching a wine glass in one hand and a plate piled high with food, in the other. He was wearing an ill-fitting dark suit, which had long gone out of fashion and, to my sensitive nostrils, smelt suspiciously of moth-balls. I was pretty certain no one had invited him! But what could I say? In fact, before I could say anything, he'd cantered across the room, seized my hand and with a wild look in his bleary blue eyes, assured me in an over-loud stage whisper, perfumed with garlic and alcohol,

"I had to come. Pay my respects and all that. You and I, and your poor departed husband, of course, we've all suffered because of those bloody lawyers, if you'll exchuse the expression." He hiccupped loudly: "It's up to you and me now to do something about it. We can't let them get away with it. We're in this together now. I'll be getting in touch with you again soon, I promish."

I didn't know how to reply to this extraordinary statement. I just wanted to escape as soon as possible and was grateful to be firmly whisked away by my faithful friend, Cathy.

18

A couple of young waiters and waitresses at the Eastledale Country Hotel, were hovering anxiously over the buffet tables, gathering up empty glasses and trays of left-over food, hoping the few remaining guests would take the hint that it was high time for them to leave. One of these was Arthur Blenkinsop. He was in no hurry.

He was glad he'd managed to find out about the time and place of this funeral, and thus be able to pay his respects to the widow of his deceased fellow accident victim. He'd gone to a lot of trouble preparing himself for today's occasion by rescuing an almost clean shirt from one of the piles of dirty laundry and by taking his best dark suit out of the storage trunk. He had decided that it could hang in the wardrobe at the end of the day, ready for some other special occasion, like going on a date with a new bird, now that he'd cleared out most of Ethel's clothes.

Arthur had really enjoyed himself today and so had Scruff, who had been thoughtfully provided by one dog-loving waitress with a bowl of drinking water. Arthur's attention had been captivated by one of the guests, a most attractive red-head. He had not noticed, however, that whenever her wine-glass had been constantly refilled by an over-attentive waiter, she had surreptitiously disposed of the contents of her glass into Scruff's drinking bowl, which he had immediately lapped up with great enthusiasm. Scruff was now underneath the buffet table, snoring gently and no doubt happily dreaming pleasant doggy dreams.

By way of contrast, Arthur was feeling more wide awake than he had done for some time. Not that he had socialised much with any of the others who were there. They were not the sort to be regulars at his local Braziers' Arms. They all looked a bit too toffee-nosed for his liking. Stuck-up lot! Although, he would have liked to get to know that dishy red-head somewhat better. She looked a bit of all right, she did. And he thought she must have taken quite a fancy to Scruff from the way that dog had been gazing up at her with adoring, expectant eyes before he disappeared under the table.

What was that saying? 'Love my dog, love me?' or something like that. Now that he was more or less a free man, he could start to think about women again, Arthur told himself. He had sidled up to the dishy red-head several times to try and ask her for her phone number, without success. Then, just as he was finally about to get to speak to her and introduce himself, one of the toffee-nosed brigade had button-holed her at the crucial moment and whisked her away. So he hadn't even had a chance to find out her full name, blast it – apart from hearing her addressed as 'Sa-a-ndra da-hrling!' Oh well, maybe he'd run across her somewhere or other when he was walking Scruff, in Friargate Passage at a later date. Or maybe he'd run into her sometime down at the Library which was nearby. She looked like the sort of woman who might read a lot. He could chat her up then, especially as she seemed to have already taken such a fancy to Scruff.

He would also have liked to talk to that gorgeous blonde bit who must be a relative or close friend of Mrs. Prettiflower, because she was constantly at her side. Mrs. Prettiflower, herself, wasn't looking too bad either, in the circumstances. Black really suited her. He'd tried without success to catch her eye several times to give her a friendly wink or a nod. He thought it might cheer her up. Show her that he was 'on her side' so to speak. But at least he had managed to say a few words to her just before she left.

He'd certainly be seeing a lot more of her soon now, when they got together to plan their case against those murderers, Smethers and Lybrand. He was looking forward to getting to know her better and even perhaps that sexy blonde as well. Maybe, to break the ice, he'd invited them both out for a drink in the Braziers' Arms, or that posh new wine bar in town, which was probably more their style.

"Funny really, when you come to think about it," he mused, "that Fate should have brought us together like that."

After all, he reminded himself again, now that he was more or less single, who knows what the future might hold?

"Have you finished with that, sir?"

Some supercilious young upstart of a waiter was practically snatching the glass out of his hand! Young people these days – no proper respect for their elders and betters. No manners, either. Selfish too, the whole lot of them. It was the parents' fault. Thatcher's children, that what they were.

"No, I haven't and I'd like a refill, if you don't mind."

"Certainly sir. *If* there's any wine left. And perhaps you'd like a doggy bag as well, sir."

The sarcasm was quite lost on Arthur, who nodded enthusiastically. This wasn't such a bad lad, after all.

"Yes, pity to waste all those chicken legs, and tasty tit-bits. I'll take them home with me for my Scruff's supper, if you'll oblige me with a doggy bag for 'em, young man."

Arthur reached across the table to reload his plate with as much of the remaining food as possible, whilst waiting for the promised doggy bag to appear, which, of course, it didn't. No problem. Arthur fished out of his pocket the two plastic bags into which he'd transferred the moth balls before setting out that morning. Congratulating himself on being thus so well prepared, he crammed both bags with enough chicken legs, sandwiches and savouries to feed himself and Scruff for a couple of meals at least. He was the last to leave, much to the relief of the catering staff, who had other pressing duties to attend to in preparing for a party of some hundred or so guests due to arrive at any moment for the wedding reception booked for that evening in their main Rainbow Restaurant.

When Arthur Blenkinsop with Scruff finally arrived back at Priory Terrace, after making his customary stop at the Braziers' Arms, he was vaguely aware in the dim street lighting that there was what appeared to be a police car parked in front of his house. This was unusual. Nothing to do with him. He supposed teenage vandals had been at it again, spraying graffiti on the Patels' side wall, no doubt. About time the police did something about it!

You never ever saw a bobby on the beat these days. Law and order just didn't seem to exist any more. Although that Tony Blair and his lot talked a lot about it. Things were no better now that they were in power than when that Maggie Thatcher was ruling the country. Not that he'd voted for any of her lot. Not like Ethel. She was an ardent supporter of Maggie Thatcher. Even though, much to her regret, Ethel couldn't personally vote for that redoubtable lady herself, she always did the next best thing by putting her cross on the ballot paper next to the name of Ernest Sprightly, the callow young Conservative candidate for their constituency. Arthur had constantly tried to tell her that Sprightly hadn't a snowflake's chance in Hell of being elected in that staunchly Labour-supporting area but Ethel took no notice. Arthur hated all politicians. Power-mad the lot of them. They didn't really care about ordinary blokes like him and all the others who had been made redundant by Bowyers Pharmaceuticals.

"Mr. Blenkinsop? Mr. Arthur Blenkinsop?"

His rambling thoughts were sharply interrupted by one of the two individuals who had climbed out of the parked police car. Both of them were now waving some kind of plastic identity cards at him. How was he expected to read them in this rotten light? It suddenly dawned on him that they had probably come to make official enquiries about his unfortunate accident, his and Scruff's that is, not forgetting that poor Mr. Prettiflower too, of course. Well they couldn't very well interview *him*. Not now, not after the poor bloke had been so recently cremated, could they?

"Yes. That's right. Arthur Blenkinsop. That's me. I've just come back from his funeral party," he added helpfully.

"Oh yes? Have you, sir?"

"Yes," Arthur belched windily, "gave him a right good send off .Did him proud, she did."

"You don't say so, sir?"

" Well, we'd like you to answer a few questions for us, if you don't mind, sir."

"Oh yes, of course. More than glad to help with your enquiries, officer."

Arthur was rather pleased with himself for using what he thought was the appropriate response, picked up from watching various detective programmes on TV. He supposed they were plain-clothes officers, since neither was in uniform. He was also still feeling euphoric after today's events. As far as he could see, everything was moving along very nicely in the right direction.

" Right then. We'd like you to come down to the station with us now, sir."

Much to the surprise and disappointment of Ruby Kersley,

who had been keeping watch for some time from the window of her cold, unlit bedroom in anticipation of witnessing a scene of high drama, Arthur Blenkinsop now that he'd come home at long last, was escorted to the waiting car without any kind of protest or fuss whatsoever. They hadn't even put handcuffs on him! It was all much too amicable as far as she could make out. Arthur slid confidently into the back seat of the car, and was on his way to the local police station in a matter of minutes. They'd even taken that wretched dog of his with them!

So great was her disappointment that real life did not resemble any incident she had seen on TV involving the arrest of a dangerous criminal, she had firmly closed her bedroom curtains, put on an extra cardigan over her nightie, filled a couple of hot water bottles and gone straight to bed. She did not, therefore, observe the return of a dazed and dishevelled Arthur Blenkinsop in the small hours of the following morning.

Scruff, too, on their return, was looking rather the worse for wear. All this to-ing and fro-ing to strange places! After all that food and delicious drink he'd been given earlier on that day, he wasn't quite sure where he was. Not only that, harsh words had been said about him at the police station when, for want of a better place to urgently relieve himself, he had peed on the corner of the official filing cabinet. What was a dog supposed to do whilst those men were yap-yapping away at one another and ignoring his pressing needs? He'd never understand the weird ways of these humans!

Arthur had been dismayed and appalled by the relentless questioning he had undergone in the last few hours. *He'd* done his best to be helpful and they had been quite attentive at first, leading him on to tell them everything. He told them of his suspicions about those two randy lawyers – that Smethers and Lybrand, and how one of them, or both of them were trying to murder him.

"Oh, and what makes you think that, sir?"

"Well you see, I was pretty certain they were up to something so I'd written to them, warning them it had got to stop."

Although all his letters had been carefully disguised as having been sent by 'a well wisher', now was the time, Arthur decided to come out of the closet, so to speak, and reveal all.

"What exactly was *it*, that had to stop?"

" Well you know…" Arthur found it embarrassing to talk about such things but it had to be said, "The hanky-panky they were getting up to with my wife, I wasn't having it any more…"

"Ah, *your wife!*"

Looks were exchanged between the officers on the other side of the table, as if to say 'now we're getting somewhere!'

"Your wife – Mrs. Ethel Blenkinsop, is that correct?"

"Yes. Quite correct."

Why this interest in Ethel? He didn't much care for the sudden steely gleam in the eyes of his chief questioner, the over-weight bald-headed geyser with a moustache, or the way in which he was leaning across the table, head thrust forward, moustache bristling in a most hostile fashion.

"And where is she now, your lady wife?"

Both his questioners were giving him their fullest attention now. Arthur did not care for the way in which they were both staring at him.

"Well how should I know! She's sure to be down under by now."

"*Down under?* You did say *down under*, didn't you, sir?"

Arthur was thoroughly irritated by this line of questioning. They were getting away from the main point. God! These cops were thick as two planks! Didn't they understand plain English? He'd better spell it out to them.

"In Australia, if you must know. I imagine," he added

sarcastically, "that's where you'll find her if you really want to go looking for her."

He hadn't come here to talk about Ethel! He was impatient to tell them all about his suspicions regarding those bloody lawyers. That's what they should really be discussing with him. Ethel was past history, as far as he was concerned.

The police officers, however, seemed to think differently. They just went on and on, asking him bloody stupid questions about Ethel. When had he last seen her? Had they had a quarrel? And had he hit her?

Well, yes he had. "But not all that hard," he added.

"And then what happened?"

"She just went. That's all."

She just went. That was all. Everything was being carefully recorded by the younger of his two questioners, the baby-faced one, and Arthur was becoming more and more agitated as the questioning went on and on. They wanted to know what clothes she was wearing when she left and what clothes she had taken with her. Well, how was he supposed to know that? He had not taken much interest in what she was wearing since those early 'turn-on' days when she wore those briefest of brief mini-skirts and stiletto heels, resulting in the unfortunate conception of Sharon, Hetty, Agnes, Gertrude.

Now they were asking him,

"And what exactly was in the large plastic sack you placed in your dustbin after your wife, as you say, *went*?"

So that's what all this was about! That bloody, nosey old cow at number 9 had been spying on him. And it must have been her who had brought about this terrible situation he was now in! It was her who had grassed on him. None of her business what he put in his dustbin. She, not him, should be the one to be under questioning for spying on her neighbours. That's what should be regarded as a crime, shouldn't it? Arthur was fuming with rage. Just let her wait until he got his hands on her. He'd…he'd…

"Answer the question, would you? What was in that sack?"

"Just bloody clothes. Her bloody clothes. That's all! Ethel wasn't going to need them where she'd gone."

"I see, there were *bloody clothes* in the sack, were there?"

"Yes! Clothes."

"*Bloody clothes*, I think you said. Correct me, if I'm wrong."

Oh God. It was a nightmare. The questioning went on and on until finally, and somewhat surprisingly to the now completely disorientated Arthur, he was allowed to leave the police station, having been warned, however, not even to think about leaving the area, as he could be called upon again at any time, pending further enquiries.

To crown it all, they had given Arthur the distinct impression that they did not believe a word he'd said when he tried tell them how he suspected that Smethers or Lybrand was trying to murder him because one or other, or possibly both of them, were having hanky-panky with his wife.

"Highly unlikely, sir," the fat moustachioed one had smirked, "since both of those gentlemen are dead."

Dead! They were dead? Both of them? Well, didn't that show that if it wasn't one of them, then there must be someone else, a serial killer, in that office and it was a good thing Ethel wasn't there any more. This was much more serious than he'd thought!

And it didn't look as if the police intended to do anything about it. So, if they weren't going to take any action, he, Arthur Blenkinsop, bloody well would!

19

It was some time after Marcus's funeral, I was at my writing desk in the sitting room, looking through the stacks of post and papers that had accumulated over the past few days.

There were an astonishing number of letters of condolence and cards from people I thought Marcus and I barely knew but who, from the glowing tributes expressed, must have known Marcus really well and held him in the highest regard. Why can't people say all these things whilst one is still alive, I wondered.

There was a most touching message which had been sent with a very grand bouquet of lilies and evergreen leaves, tied with purple satin ribbon from some firm of solicitors, Messrs. Smethers and Lybrand. I suppose I was still in a bemused state of shock because I was wondering how it was that Marcus had come to know them. I came to the conclusion that it must be through some aspect of his work he had come into contact with them, as we still retained our old friend, Ben Hudson, in London as our legal adviser.

Then of course I remembered! Smethers and Lybrand's offices were in Friargate Passage, nearby to where Marcus had received that dreadful blow on his head. How thoughtful of them! I must write and thank them for their concern.

However, I suddenly remembered something else, or rather, someone else – that peculiar man, Arthur something-or-other, who kept popping up everywhere I went, or so it seemed – first at the hospital and then again at Marcus's funeral, with his dog! Not that I had been able to take in much of what he said at the time, he'd maintained that someone at Smethers and Lybrand was trying to kill *him* by hurling a gigantic cheese at him and that the fatal blow to the head Marcus had accidentally received had really been meant for *him*. How ridiculous, I remember thinking at the time, even if someone had been trying to kill that irritating Arthur Thingummy, they certainly wouldn't have chosen a cheese as a murder weapon, now would they?

★★★

"Strike while the iron's hot," Cathy had said to me.

It's a cliché, I know, but rather appropriate in this northern setting where continual hammering and welding is such an important part of the industrial process. What she actually meant was that I should renew regular contact right away with Liz Marley.

"Show her that you are seriously working again now. Ideas bubbling away in the melting pot. And that you're not just doing an 'Irish'".

"Doing an Irish?" I bristled. Great story-tellers the Irish and I like to think I have some drops of creative Irish blood in my veins, inherited from my maternal great-grandfather who, it was said, lived to be nearly a hundred years old and was something of a story-teller. He claimed not only to have shaken the hand of that great literary genius, W. B. Yeats, but also to have kissed the original blarney stone. Well, I suppose if you reach that age, you are entitled to claim anything you like! All the same, I was ready to defend my ancestral roots against any adverse criticism.

"Yes. *Some*, I'm not saying all," replied Cathy, sensing my raw-nervedness, "spend more time talking about what they're going to write than actually doing it."

"Oh! Well yes. I know what you mean," I said and let it pass, having met people of many ethnic backgrounds who practised this particular form of inventiveness in all kinds of ways.

Anyway, that was how I came to ring Liz again a few weeks after the funeral, as a follow-up to my first call. It was a pity I didn't actually get to speak to Liz because Cathy had really inspired me with some of her ideas, impressing upon me the value of starting a new chapter in my own life now that the earlier chapters in which Marcus had played a major part had come to an end.

20

Intermission

I really hadn't expected to hear from Margot Prettiflower again, and certainly not that soon anyway. At least this time my voice-mail was switched on, so I didn't have to talk to her, only listen to her long and incoherent message at the end of my long and trying day. As it was, there were stacks of manuscripts still to be dealt with piled up on my desk, My diary was choc-a-block with appointments for the forthcoming weeks and, I had other worries on my mind of a more personal nature.

Alex and I were going through a particularly difficult patch in our relationship. His bitch of a wife was, according to Alex, refusing to listen to any mention of divorce on religious grounds, which sounded a bit thin to me because I'm pretty certain that she's not Catholic. Alex certainly isn't. And, he's been behaving oddly ever since he got back from Frankfurt. I've scarcely seen him. He didn't come round for our romantic dinner à deux. Pressure of work, he says, working all hours God sends. Well, I know only too well what that's like. It's pretty hectic here too. On the other hand, there's a nagging suspicion at the back of my mind that all is not well, apart from the problems over that wife of his. There's something he's not telling me.

And there was that infuriating Margot Prettiflower burbling away about Cathy Goodson having given her a make-over after the funeral.

The funeral? Whose funeral, for God's' sake? I'd thought she was the one who'd died but of course, it wasn't. And what was all that about a make-over? What on earth was she on about?

I knew she and Cathy Goodson were friends, which is how Margot was introduced to me in the first place. Cathy is one of 'my' authors and very pleased I am to have her on our lists. So I tried to listen to Margot's seemingly endless soliloquy. From what I could gather, Cathy's make-over treatment had transformed Margot so completely that Margot was thinking of adopting a nom-de-plume, like Marie Gold, and dropping her surname.

'Solely for my adult writing and for the brand new born-again me,' she said.

She wanted to know what I thought about it. Jesus! Had she gone all religious? I wondered where all this was leading, especially when she then went on about Cathy's encouragement to seriously consider sex in relation to the older generation, especially for women because they read more books than men, she said.

Well! The mind boggles. Why ask me? I really didn't want to know what she and Cathy were getting up to. That's something strictly between themselves. Unless, of course, Cathy was thinking about using it in her next book, in which case it would more than likely be very marketable, with her name on the cover. Her books are extremely popular with library users and librarians too.

They are, on the whole, much more broad-minded about what they put on their fiction shelves these days. Not just in the realms of adult fiction but in the children's section too — Big Ears and little Noddy have once again been sitting comfortably for some time now upon the shelves in most libraries. But, as far as Margot Prettiflower was concerned…I just couldn't imagine what she had in mind. In my professional opinion, she really should stick to Pinkie the Elephant.

21

"Don't you want to know more about Marcus's accident?" Cathy had asked me, when, much later, she heard that according to the Coroner's Report, it was caused by 'an unidentified object from an unknown source'.

"No. Not really, Cathy."

I was profoundly grateful that I had been spared the necessity of attending the Coroner's Court, and having to listen to all the distressing details. I couldn't have faced that. At that time, I accepted the fact that it was up to the Coroner to determine the cause of death. As I said at the beginning, all the details surrounding Marcus's death were not known to me then. The reality was that no matter what the circumstances were, he had been suddenly taken from me. There was nothing I, or anyone else could do to change that.

"It happened, Cathy. Marcus is dead. Nothing can change that now. Nothing's going to bring Marcus back to me, is it?"

"No, but what are you going to do about that scruffy dog man? He's bound to turn up yet again. What are you going to do if he bothers you again?"

"Oh, I'll cope," I promised, trying to sound more confident than I actually felt. "I'll think of something to get rid of him."

"Of course you will!" Cathy agreed, rather too enthusiastically I thought. "Besides, you'll be able to contact me at the touch of a button, by e-mailing me, once you get going on your new computer."

I really wasn't too sure about this changeling electronic brain-child which Cathy had insisted upon introducing into my household, as all part of the 'Margot make-over plan'. My trusty old typewriter having now been consigned to the forthcoming scouts' jumble sale. It had been a painful parting. It was like rejecting an old friend. I was sorely tempted to go to the scouts' jumble sale and buy it back again but some burly boy scout's Dad would no doubt have beaten me to it. So I would have no option but to get to know how to operate this one-eyed monster which Cathy had foisted upon me, with its bewildering keyboard and most un-mouse like mouse.

"You'll love it once you've got the hang of it," she assured me. "I write all my books on mine. Couldn't manage without it now. You'll be working again in no time, you'll see."

Now gazing out of the sitting-room window, I was thinking with an aching sense of loss, how cold and bleak the garden looked. Although the snow had almost disappeared, except for one or two small patches under the hawthorn hedges, I was longing for the time when signs of renewed life would begin to appear. Cathy, who had urgent deadlines to deal with to meet the demands of her current publisher, was leaving that day, which was another reason for feeling sad.

" Oh Cathy!" I sighed. "Spring is such a long time coming to these frozen northerly parts. Everything seems so bleak here. Eternal winter. And what *am* I going to do without you? I'm going to miss you so much."

"You won't have time to miss me," she said, thrusting a tissue into my hand, "so come on now, no more tears, duckie. You're going to be much too busy on your new computer from now on, especially when you get started working on that new chapter in your life. Just remember, Spring always comes after Winter, and Spring is a beautiful new beginning."

It sounded remarkably like the title of one of her books. Cathy was a great one for making out lists and, based on all the things we'd talked about over the last few days, she'd left a pile of these lists on my writing desk. There was a lengthy one for books I could borrow from the local library, to help me researching into the kind of writing she was urging me to pursue now. Titles such as *Burning with Desire, Made for Love, Knights of Passion, Mistresses and Masters*. Not at all the kind of thing I would have read previously, but she and I had soon found after much discussion that there were glaring gaps in my background knowledge as to how to approach sex in a way which would interest the reader of today's adult fiction. I'd never had to think about this in connection with *Pinkie the Elephant*, for whom despite all his exciting adventures, sex was an unexplored territory.

"The best kind of writing comes from your own personal experience," Cathy had so rightly said. No wonder she was so successful with such a rich and varied experience to draw upon. She had been so much more adventurous than I.

"Or," she added kindly noting my worried expression, "by thoroughly researching your subject matter."

My mother had studiously avoided the subject of love-making or 'sex' as it is now referred to, hoping Marcus would provide all the instruction required to fulfil my wifely role in every sense of the word. So when Marcus and I married, I'd had practically no preparation for sex within marriage, let alone out of it.

You couldn't glean very much from books or magazines in those pre-permissive days either, not like it is now. And even sneaky peeks into that then forbidden classic, *Lady Chatterley's Lover*, didn't really offer any sensible and practical instruction on the matter. All that cavorting about naked in the rain, didn't sound like much fun to me when, years later I got around to reading this daring literary work.

There were certainly no books available from the public lending libraries then either, and it was a much neglected subject in other publications of that era, as far as I was aware. Although, I seem to remember there were carefully worded advertisements in certain magazines for books with coy titles like *Married Love* to be sent for through the post, and which arrived in tightly sealed discreet brown paper packages.

As Philip Larkin maintained in his *Annus Mirabilis*:

"Sexual intercourse began in nineteen sixty-three/ (Which was rather late for me) Between the end of the Chatterley ban/And the Beatles' first L.P."

The house was strangely silent now that Cathy had gone. Her parting words to me had been,

"Get started on that new chapter right now, Margot Prettiflower. This is to be your renaissance remember. And I want regular updates on your progress. So don't you forget it. You can do that by emailing me. No excuses mind."

"I won't, I promise," I called as she climbed into that ridiculously improbable yellow Citroen of hers.

I walked back into my writing corner in the sitting room and sat down at my desk to study the various lists she had left for me.

"Let's see," I said to myself, glancing at the list on the top of the pile, headed *Margot's To Do List*, "Well, I can forget that one for a start."

I picked up a pencil and crossed off 'Join local health club'. Whatever was she thinking of? Neither of us had been any good at sport in our school-days, which admittedly were a good few years ago. So what was the point of this particular 'to do' item? She had put a star beside this suggestion too, and others on the list. So what did that mean? As a footnote explanation of the star symbol she had written 'possible venue for meeting members of the opposite sex'.

"Oh for Heaven's sake, Cathy!"

I drew another pencil line firmly through this item. This was definitely not for me. Unlike Cathy, I would not be actively seeking a new partner in a health club or anywhere else for that matter. Besides, the mere thought of so much wobbly sweaty flesh straining away to achieve a body beautiful, under the illusion that you can somehow cheat Nature and Old Father Time, was definitely offputting.

So offputting in fact that I felt in urgent need of a reinvigorating cup of tea, especially after glancing at the second item on the list – 'becoming familiar with your computer'. That was scary – getting acquainted with this new-fangled form of communication, even though as Cathy pointed out that from now on I would be in regular contact with her and Liz Marley. I had an uneasy feeling this was not going to be all plain sailing. There would be stormy seas ahead for me in this uncharted territory.

22

Ruby Kersley was all of a-tremble. She was surprised that the police had allowed that awful neighbour of hers, Arthur Blenkinsop, to come home. Him being a wife-killer and all that, or at least wife-abductor, because Ethel certainly wasn't around any more now, was she?

Ruby had realised Arthur Blenkinsop was back again the next morning when, from behind her lace curtains, she saw him with that scruffy dog of his going past her house. He was glaring up at her windows with a right murderous expression on his face. Quick as greased lightning, she darted back from her window. But he must have seen her because he made one of those obscene gestures at her – that sign road-raged men use when threatening other road-users!

Oh Gawd! She didn't feel safe, living so close to him, especially now he was on the loose again. He might be one of those serial killers, like that Jack the Ripper. As a great reader of crime fiction, she'd read all about him and his victims. All women they were. And there were lots of other men just like him. She'd read about them, too, in the newspaper. Men who lured innocent women into their clutches and then did away with them. *She* could be next on his list! What was she going to do?

She'd move out. Go and stay with her cousin Mabel, that's what. At least for a few days until the police came back to arrest him properly. Shakily she climbed on a chair, took down her suitcase from the top of the wardrobe and started to pack hastily. She needn't take much – just her winceyette nightie, bedsocks, cardigan, and a couple of pairs of her warm winter knickers. As a young girl, she had been always told to make sure she had a spare pair of clean knickers handy with strong elastic, so as not to be caught out in an emergency. Two extra pairs should be enough. Maybe she could sneak back home some time later to snatch up a further change of clothes, if needs be.

In any case, she must leave enough room in her suitcase for dear Fred. She'd not leave *him* behind, at the mercy of any vandals who might break in and steal all her valuables while she was away from home. True she was insured, but then she'd never understood the small print in the policy the Pru had sent her. So she might well not be covered for the loss of Fred. In that case, she couldn't risk leaving him behind. Besides, some things were irreplaceable even under the Pru's generous assurance to replace 'new-for-old'. It would just not be possible to replace her dear departed Fred. Not in the same condition as he was in now anyway.

She could, of course, Ruby supposed, with the insurance money get another of them fancy urns from the undertakers but it was what was inside this one that was so important to her. They would not be able to replace her dear Fred's ashes, now would they? And no way would she be willing to accept any kind of substitute.

Pondering thus, Ruby, carefully and lovingly, took down from the shelf over the fireplace, the expensively ornate urn in which her late husband, or rather his ashes, had rested ever since his demise from lung cancer.

She had missed Fred's actual physical presence when he'd first passed away. Even though there was less work for her after he'd gone. No longer did she have to empty all those overflowing ashtrays, Fred having been a forty-a-day man. He had never been much of a conversationalist when he was around, which was one of the things she loved most about him. She'd always found him to be such a good listener. Never interrupting her, apart from a wheezy grunt now and then, when she was telling him the latest juiciest bits of local gossip. And, above all, he'd never laid a finger on her. No, not ever. Not like some husbands she could mention. He'd been a good man and a good husband, her Fred.

"I'd not go anywhere without you, not ever, my lovie," she murmured softly, as she gave the urn a quick dust and polish over, before placing it tenderly in her suitcase. It fitted in snugly between her winceyette nightie and her warm winter knickers.

She didn't yet know how long she might have to stay with Mabel. At least until 'that man' next door was safely under lock and key! So perhaps she ought to take some foodstuff with her too. After all, Mabel wasn't expecting her and even if she were, she never kept much in her meagre larder apart from some unappetising left-overs, like the remains of tinned sardines, days' old cottage pie or cold cauliflower cheese. Mabel liked cheese and so did Ruby, who was far from keen on the sardines or the stale cottage pie.

"I know what I'll do," Ruby decided in a sudden burst of generosity, "I'll take her some of that special cheese I found in the market. That'll be a bit of a treat for her."

She had been delighted with the cheese she had bought quite recently from a rather shifty-looking stall-holder in the market. Ruby had a nose for a good bargain and it was lucky she happened to spot that cheese before the stall holder disappeared. He appeared to be in a great hurry to clear his stall and was selling off his stock at remarkably low prices.

"Last you through to next Christmas, that will, petal," he'd said to her with a wink as he cut her a generous chunk. Don't often see cheese like this these days, do you now?"

It was undeniably one of the most unusual cheeses she'd seen in a long time.

With the cheese now in her suitcase, carefully gift-wrapped in some Christmas paper she'd saved from one of the Christmas presents she'd received, and painstakingly ironed, Ruby was making her way cautiously out of her house, just as Arthur Blenkinsop was coming out of his front door. Oh Gawd! Had he seen her? What should she do now? Retreat indoors? Not on your life! She'd better make a run for it.

Firmly clutching her suitcase, she scurried off down the length of Priory Terrace like a frightened old fowl who had just caught wind of a prowling fox. She arrived at her cousin Mabel's house in such a flustered state that it took nearly a whole bottle of Mabel's post-Christmas sweet sherry to calm the nerves of both these ladies, who then enjoyed a very merry evening together watching a horror movie on TV.

★★★

Arthur Blenkinsop had been blissfully unaware of the agitation he had aroused in the bosom of Ruby Kersley. Out of the corner of his eye he thought he had seen her scuttling away but he wasn't entirely sure.

He wondered if he needed glasses or if those pills the doctor had prescribed for his nerves were making him see and feel all peculiar. At the same time, he had once again marvelled at how fast Ruby Kersley could move with that dodgy hip of hers – silly old bitch! At her age, she shouldn't be rushing about like that. She should be taking things quietly at her time of life. Anyway, no time to waste his precious thoughts on *her*. He had more important matters on his mind.

It wasn't until a couple of days later that he put on his

best suit again with a brand-new piece of blue toilet tissue carefully folded and placed in the breast-pocket. He needed to look his best, he told himself, to pursue his plan for further action.

After his upsetting encounter with the police, Arthur had hardly set foot out-of-doors, except for a quick visit to the chemist's for more of his nerve pills and on to the off-licence to pick up a bottle of whisky to 'help the medicine go down'.

He hadn't even felt like dropping in for his usual pint at the Braziers' Arms. The chaotic state of his house was beginning to thoroughly depress him. What with those piles of unwashed laundry, the stacks of dirty crockery and that awful smell in the kitchen – it was enough to make any man feel down-right depressed.

Today, however, the appearance of watery winter sunshine had helped cheer him up somewhat and strengthen his resolve to put unpleasant memories firmly behind him. He told himself not to dwell on what had happened to Ethel. What was done couldn't be undone.

It was time to move on and think about the future now that he was more or less single again. He'd probably be quite well-off too, once he got his compensation claim against those bloody lawyers settled. He really should be thinking about finding a new woman in his life to take Ethel's place. She'd soon tidy the place up again for him. After all, he had a nice comfortable three-up-and-two-down home to offer some lucky female *and,* there wouldn't be the pressing need to marry the next one, as there had been with Ethel. He'd make sure of that this time.

He studied himself carefully in the hall mirror. His suit, which had lost most of its clinging aroma of moth-balls – not that Arthur himself had ever noticed *that* – had been carefully ironed by him earlier that morning, together with a blue and white striped shirt, he'd rescued from the pile of unwashed clothes on the bedroom floor.

"Looking quite good," he decided, nodding his approval at his reflection in the mirror, after twisting and turning to see if the scorch marks on the trouser crotch from the over-heated iron showed at all.

He'd even added a piece of folded blue soft-as-silk toilet tissue to his breast pocket, in the style of HRH Prince Charles. The only difference between him and HRH being that HRH's would, of course, be a fine linen handkerchief, loving well laundered either by that new bird of his or by one of his many minions. Nevertheless, Arthur prided himself on the resemblance. In fact Ethel, in the days when she had taken more notice of Arthur, had often commented on the likeness in appearance of these two men – except for the ears. Arthur's being smaller and sexier, according to Ethel.

"And if *He*," concluded Arthur, with a final adjustment to the breast pocket arrangement, "can net a second bird to comfort him in his latter years, then why shouldn't I?"

Arthur's destination was to the Central Library, having, after much thought, come to the decision that his forthcoming battle with Messrs. Smethers and Lybrand would be carried out by himself alone. *He* wasn't going to spend his good money on lawyers. They were all rogues, the whole lot of them.

He, himself, he decided, could find out all he needed to know about legal matters from books in the public library. After all, that's what libraries were for, weren't they, to assist members of the public in the pursuit of knowledge? That's what he'd paid his taxes for, all those years he'd slaved away as a wage-earner at Bowyers Pharmaceuticals. Not only that, but he'd noticed when he'd been walking Scruff in Friargate Passage that apart from OAPs, quite a few dishy, classy-looking birds seemed to frequent the library.

He'd take Scruff with him. Smarten him up a bit, ready for some chance encounter. It was a well-known fact that a person walking a dog or pushing a pram could readily get into conversation with a complete stranger. Women loved cooing over strange babies and dogs. For instance, there was that gorgeous red-head who'd shown such an interest in Scruff at his fellow victim's funeral party. Who knows, he might even run across her again. Buoyed up with this happy thought, he set off towards the library.

Having located the appropriate section and spotted on the shelves several useful titles such as *Be your own Lawyer, Law made Easy for Everyone,* and *The Simple Man's Guide to the Law,* Arthur settled himself down to make notes from these erudite volumes on the scraps of paper he drew from his pocket. It was not as easy as he had imagined. The text, on the whole read too much like legal jargon to be easily assimilated.

He was having great difficulty in understanding some pages relating to personal injury claims, which had more to do with road accidents, injuries in factories, and warehouses and at work, than his particular circumstances, when he was suddenly aware of some kind of disturbance at the library reception counter.

Nigel Hirst, the librarian and leading tenor in his local church choir, was answering a telephone call. His voice, raised to almost falsetto surprise, resounding clearly throughout the library, was asking,

"You did say *'sex'*, didn't you, Mrs. Prettiflower? You want *'everything to do with sex'*, you said. Well, it's a bit of a tall order, but if you'd care to look in sometime later on this week, I'll certainly see what I can do for you."

Arthur Blenkinsop was amazed by what he had just heard. That Mrs. Prettiflower, of all people! And her husband not yet cold in his grave, or more accurately, cooled in his urn because the poor bastard had only just been cremated, hadn't he?

He'd gathered, from snippets of conversation overheard in the Braziers' Arms from time to time, that widow women were sometimes taken this way. 'Up for it' was the expression they'd used. He would never have thought it though of Mrs. Prettiflower. She didn't look like that kind of woman – not really what you'd call 'sexy' by any stretch of the imagination. Although, come to think of it, she wasn't looking too bad at her husband's funeral party. Perhaps she was like the widows referred to in the Braziers' Arms making preparations to be 'up for it'. Well, she certainly hadn't wasted much time!

Yes, on second thoughts, perhaps he would ask her out. Do her a favour like. After all, he had good reasons for contacting her, didn't he? She wasn't really his type, but at least she was available, after what had happened to her husband. *Very* available from the sound of it, too! Now, if she'd been more like that gorgeous red-head with the legs, or even more like a younger version of his Ethel…Phew! That would be quite something!

His Ethel? He told himself she wasn't 'his' any longer. He must stop thinking about her. She was no longer part of his life. He really should be concentrating on finding a new woman to take her place. He desperately needed a woman – someone to clean up a bit around the house, make him a few decent meals and get rid of that awful smell in the kitchen now that Ethel wasn't there any more.

But first, he'd have to make a bit of an effort to win that Mrs. Prettiflower over, like buying her a drink or two. Start by taking her some flowers perhaps, nothing too fancy or expensive though. Women liked flowers. There was that red-flowering potted plant thing which Ethel had put in the dining room sometime before Christmas, he could take her that. It had lost a few of its leaves but he supposed it would freshen up with a drop of something or other. Few drops of that whisky he'd just bought? Well, perhaps not. Why waste good booze on a plant. *She'*d most likely know what to do with it. Women were better at that sort of thing than men. He'd ask her out and if things went really well, he'd even ask his doctor to add that Putiteg drug to his prescription, so that he'd be prepared not to disappoint her.

He'd go round to her house later on today, when he'd finished looking things up in the library. He'd even offer, he thought magnanimously, to do all the paperwork for her in presenting their claim jointly to Smethers & Lybrand. She probably didn't know much about how to put things in writing. So she'd, no doubt, be suitably grateful, and want to show him her appreciation, especially when the financial compensation was paid out, if not before.

23

I had not been sleeping well, waking in the wintry darkness of early morning and reaching out to touch cold empty nothingness. My darling Marcus, my dearest one and only love, was no longer there beside me. I was angry that he had been taken from me by such a cruel stroke of Fate. Tears which had not been shed in public, now overwhelmed me. I was angry then with myself for stupid, futile self-pity. Tears were not going to bring Marcus back to me.

Will we ever be reunited, he and I, in the great Hereafter, wherever or whatever that is? Who knows? That's even more uncertain than life itself. It's a question which none of us, whatever our beliefs, can really answer. There may be a Heaven. Most of us live in the hope that there is. And there might be Hell – which doesn't bear thinking about. But there is this Earth. And the certainty of that is that I *am* here and now upon this earth. Undeniably I exist, and therefore I am.

"So, think positive, Margot Prettiflower," I urged myself, "the sooner you get started on the new era in your life, the better."

There was that long 'To do' list which Cathy had made out for me, lying on my desk, wasn't there? I was toying with the idea of getting out of bed and going downstairs to take another look at it, when sleep overcame me at last bringing with it a strange and ridiculous dream.

I was in my nightdress, walking along a narrow ill-lit passageway, large, round yellow objects were falling all around me. I had to move carefully to avoid being hit by them or having to step on them to reach the end of the passageway where two shadowy figures were standing. The passageway became narrower and narrower. It was closing in on me. There was no turning back. As I got closer to them, I recognised who they were. It was that annoying scruffy-dog man, Arthur Blenkinsop, and his dog. He was leering at me with those ghastly yellow teeth and his scruffy dog was barking loudly.

I tried to shout "Shut up! Go away!" but no sound would come from my dry mouth.

It was a nightmare. They were coming towards me. Arthur Blenkinsop's bleary blue eyes were fixed upon me now in a glassy, menacing, stare, as they drew closer and closer. I felt trapped to the point of screaming "No, no, no! Go away!" Then I woke up.

"That'll teach you not to eat Welsh rarebit late at night, my girl!" I told myself. You would have thought that after what had happened to Marcus, I would have been put off cheese for ever.

It was Cathy's fault really. Before she left, she had restocked my fridge and store cupboard for me, with 'wholesome food' like the cheese she'd bought from a stall in the market, which was remarkably good value, compared with London prices, she'd informed me. There was such a great hunk of it that she'd even taken some of it back to London with her. And I, frugal housewife that I am from my mother's training, couldn't possibly let it go to waste. Hence the cheese supper.

The doorbell was ringing insistently. Still dazed and shaking from my troubled sleep, I wondered who could be calling at such an early hour. A glance at the tiny travelling clock beside my bed however showed it was far from early. It was almost ten-thirty. *Ten-thirty*! I couldn't believe that I'd over-slept so late. Not only that, I had an appointment with Justin Walker at eleven. It was going to be a rush to get showered and dressed in time. I'd have to skip breakfast.

Justin had been coming on a regular basis now, helping me to get to grips with this new-fangled computer, which Cathy had insisted I acquire immediately, as soon as she'd discovered that he was such an expert in these matters. I was beginning to find that Justin was really charming and a very good teacher. He told me I was a fast learner. Mother would have been proud of me. She would have been glad to know that my early training at that expensive secretarial college had paid off! Tackling the use of the keyboard had therefore not so far presented any problems but there were other aspects of making fuller use of this dreaded machine which I had yet to learn.

Today, Justin was going to initiate me into the mysteries of surfing the net and emailing, which he assured me I was going to find fantastically useful. Not that I had the addresses of many people to email as yet, only Cathy's and Liz Marley's and a few of Marcus's ex-colleagues, but I daresay I'd be adding to the list before long, once I got started.

"A whole new world will be opening up for you," Justine had assured me. "Take my word for it."

After the lesson that morning, I was due to call in at the library to collect all the reference material that helpful Mr. Hirst had promised me for researching my new book. So, I had a busy day ahead of me.

The doorbell rang again, even more insistently this time.

Surely Justin hadn't arrived half an hour early! He was usually so punctual and always so immaculately dressed too. Oh Lord, what should I do now? I couldn't leave the poor man standing out there on the doorstep, in the bitter cold. He must be freezing! Without stopping to think, I dashed downstairs to let him in. It was only as I opened the front door, and felt the bite of the north-easterly wind through my flimsy nightdress, that I remembered I was still in a state of undress. And there, leering at me across the threshold and staring with those bleary blue eyes of his, like a continuation of my nightmare, stood that ghastly Arthur Blenkinsop *and* his barking, tail-wagging dog.

"I've been working on our case…" he began, "and I've brought you this for you."

He was holding one of those slippery plastic document files in one hand and a wilting poinsettia, obviously well past its survival date, in the other. These plants are forced into a glowing state of irresistible saleability in time for the Christmas market, then, poor things, they fade away and get thrown out with the discarded Christmas decorations. Cruelty to plants, I call it! Why was he bringing me this dying plant? What was I supposed to do with it? He must have observed my look of concern and bewilderment.

"Just needs a bit of tender, loving care to revive it. Like most of us," he said, with a most suggestive leer, thrusting the poinsettia into my hands. " Which reminds me," he went on, waving the document file at me, "if I could step inside, I think we should get started on this case of ours right away…"

Case? What case? What was he talking about?

Exactly what he was wanting to get started on, I didn't wait to hear.

"I'm sorry, Mr. Blenkinsop," I cut in frostily, "but it's not at all convenient right now. I'm expecting someone for a very important appointment in a few moments. So if you'll excuse me…"

He goggled at me with such a hurt expression in those bleary blue eyes of his, I couldn't help feeling a sudden surge of pity for him. He looked so miserable. I had no right to inflict the rawness of my own sense of loss on him, just because he'd turned up with that sick plant and his file of papers at an awkward time.

After all, I really knew nothing about him or what his personal circumstances were. From his garbled remarks when we first met at the hospital, I seemed to remember that he'd hinted at some recent tragedy in his own life and that he too, had undergone some traumatic experience which had severely affected his nervous system. But I really wasn't ready to take on the burden of someone else's troubles at such a time.

"I really am very sorry, Mr. Blenkinsop, but please don't call again." I said as gently as I could, hurriedly closing the front door, then dashing upstairs to dress and make myself respectable as quickly as possible for my eleven o'clock computer lesson with Justin Walker.

24

Arthur Blenkinsop stood staring at the closed front door for several moments. He was stunned not only by Margot Prettiflower's behaviour towards him but by her appearance. Bold as brass and all undressed she'd been at that time of the morning too, declaring she was expecting a caller! Brazen hussy – that's what she was. And then turning him away like that, without even taking the flowers he'd brought her, or listening to what he had to say about their claim for damages against those lawyers. Spurning his help, just like that. After all the trouble he'd been to, looking things up and everything. Ungrateful bitch! She wasn't his type anyway. She could bloody well make her own claims *if* she knew how to do it. *He* wasn't going to help her or bother with her any more, not after what he'd seen this morning.

Having come to this decision, he turned firmly away from the house and, with Scruff trotting patiently at his heels, started walking off down the gravel drive, hurling the wilting poinsettia into the herbaceous border as he went. As he did so, the plastic folder slipped from his grasp and all his carefully prepared notes went fluttering all over the drive.

"Bloody effing hell!" he groaned as he scrabbled around in a desperate attempt to retrieve his precious papers. As if things weren't bad enough already for him. He sometimes wondered if Fate didn't have it in for him, good and proper. Just because he'd been born on a Wednesday. It was an unlucky day. His old mum had always said so because it had been on a Wednesday that the dad he'd never known had gone off and left them in the lurch. And, *'Wednesday's child is full of woe'*, according to the old nursery line which he'd learnt as a child, had come back to haunt him time and time again over the years. Well he'd certainly had his share of woes throughout his life, he told himself.

He'd managed to gather his notes all together when, with a sudden screech of brakes, a red sports car appeared on the drive, almost on top of him. The driver, with great presence of mind, swerved skilfully round Arthur and Scruff. Then, with a regal wave and a cheery "So sorry, old chap!" continued blithely on towards Margot Prettiflower's front door.

One glance at the driver of the car was enough to confirm Arthur's worst suspicions. So *that* was her caller. That bloke who'd been chatting up all the best-looking birds at the funeral party! It was true then what they said in the Braziers' Arms about widow women, he thought bitterly.

He hated all women. They were the ones who'd been the cause of all the trouble in his life – his mother, for getting pregnant and bringing him into this world in the first place, then Ethel for landing him with daughter Sharon, the Personnel officer at Bowyers Pharmaceuticals for handing him his redundancy notice just before Christmas and now that Mrs. Prettiflower for the way she'd treated him just now. And he'd never felt so alone and so cold, in his life as he did at that moment.

Justin Walker, on the other hand, was feeling on top of the world. After a careful practised smile at his reflection in his windscreen mirror, a quick dab of *Harem*, the latest much-advertised, irresistible after-shave, which he always kept in his glove compartment, and a reassuring smoothing of his well-coiffured silver-grey hair, he bounded out of the car and strode confidently towards Margot's front door.

He was enjoying these teaching sessions with Margot. She was a good, conscientious learner, even though she was, like all women of a certain age, rather scared of modern technology. Justin told himself the old girl needed a new interest in her life, after losing Marcus so suddenly from some obscure disease. What was it? Ashky-something or other. It sounded very unpleasant and all very sudden too, but it wouldn't have been right for him as a gentleman to ask a grieving widow for any further details. He'd liked old Marcus. Even though he was probably Jewish. Not that Justin held that against him. Marcus was a decent sort of chap considering he wasn't English and hadn't been to any of 'the right schools' or Oxbridge, or held the rank of officer in the Army. Good bridge player though and a bit of a music buff.

Justin had not met Margot before the funeral, or if he had he couldn't really remember her. She wasn't exactly his 'little black book' material but for Marcus's sake, he'd do whatever he could to help her get over her loss. Women needed a man in their lives. He, of all people, knew that to be so. Extraordinary how Fate had brought Margot and Cathy Goodson, that gorgeous friend of hers, into his life. He'd certainly like to get to know *her* better. All in good time though. These matters shouldn't be rushed. He'd remind Margot about his offer to make use of his holiday apartment in Majorca. Casually suggest her friend might like to accompany her. No need at this stage to mention that he would also be taking a break there at the same time. It wouldn't do to scare her off.

With his hand poised over the doorbell, Justin paused momentarily to look back down the drive, catching a glimpse of the dejected receding Arthur Blenkinsop and his dog. He wondered where he'd seen them both before, but could not remember where. He also wondered what the chap was doing here today. One of those irritating down-on- their-luck door-to-door salesmen, double-glazing or something of that sort, no doubt. From the look of him, the poor chap hadn't been all that successful in whatever he had been trying to sell Margot.

25

Jesus Chr-i-st! I don't know whether I'm coming or going! Everything, but everything is weighing me down. I feel as if I'm sinking under that mountain of unread manuscripts, those piles of unanswered letters memos and 'urgent' phone calls which must be responded to. I daren't look at my engagement diary. My secretary's off sick, and so are most of the other staff with whatever brand of flu is in vogue this winter. So everyone's much too busy to lend a hand to poor, overworked me! I can't go down with flu, I just can't spare the time with all this work to be done. I have to keep going because I just can't let my authors down.

It's those emails which are really getting to me. The worst of it is, I don't know who's sending them. They're all coming in shoals from "IluvitdontU". They started off with this sort of thing: 'Sex and the older woman is astonishing, isn't it, the more you find out about it. Although I'm sure that with all your experience you'll know much more about it than I do!' Then they go on with what appear to be quotes of purple soft porn passages taken from the kind of books we ourselves would never consider submitting to any of our publishers, who value their reputations as highly as we do ours.

The most recent one ended up with 'Let's explore some more when we're out of this world in Majorca.' What the hell did that mean? Why would I be going to Majorca when I've all this work to get through?

Apart from the question of infringement of copyrights, who can be doing this to me? It couldn't be some spiteful former employee now working for a rival agency, could it? No. We all adhere to a strict Code of Conduct in our profession.

A computer virus? No. No other computer in this organisation has been affected by it. So it couldn't be that.

A mystery stalker? Sinister possibility that.

Or, it could be Alex. Former lover-boy, the rat. Hmm. The more I think about that, the more likely that possibility appears to be.

He and I had had an almighty row over this on/off divorce business. I'd told him to take his LPs, his CDs, his Thai recipe book and his dirty socks out of my flat, take them back home to his ghastly wife, or to that new tart of his, whoever she is, as I never wanted to see him again, ever. That was just after he'd got back from Venice. Oh yes – Venice – not Frankfurt where he said he was going for his business trip. How could he lie to me like that? How could he!

You can imagine how I felt when I found out about that, which is why I can't concentrate on any of this fiction stuff that's piled up all around me at the moment. What is happening to me here and now is all too real. My pain is real and, My God, after giving Alex some of the best years of my life, it hurts like Hell. And, in real life when one chapter comes to an end, starting a new one does not come easy. Not at my age. Not at any age. It's all very well to say: 'Move on. Forget him. Go and find yourself someone else.' It takes a Hell of a lot of guts and I'm not sure if I can go there. Not yet, anyway. My work is the only thing that matters to me right now. This is what brings me real fulfilment. Work will be my life and my love from now on.

26

Arthur Blenkinsop was not quite sure how he got home that particular morning. He was shaking all over. He was feeling terrible as if he was having one of those funny turns again. He wasn't sure either if he had taken his nerve pills before he went off to see that Mrs. Prettiflower. So he'd better take them as soon as he'd fed Scruff some of that bargain cheese he'd bought from the market. Good thing Scruff was the kind of dog who would eat almost anything. Besides, there wasn't anything else to feed him with in the store cupboard. Between them, they'd finished up all those goodies Arthur had brought back from that funeral party a while ago. Neither of them had been particularly bothered by the slight mothbally flavour. In fact, Arthur thought it gave the chicken legs an agreeable piquancy.

Arthur himself didn't really care that much for the cheese he'd bought from the market. But a bargain was a bargain, and he had to be careful with his money these days. That is until he collected the compensation that was definitely owing to him from those bloody lawyers, Smethers & Lybrand.

It was all there in black and white. "Special damages are payable for injuries which can be physical and/or psychological" according to that law book he'd found in the library. So there was no doubt about that. They wouldn't print something like that if it wasn't true, now would they?

He had no idea how much the settlement might be. It could

be thousands of pounds, from what he had seen headlined in the popular press. There were examples of cases where individuals, usually some money-grabbing female or other, had suffered far less psychological trauma than he and Scruff had, where they had been awarded thousands of pounds. In his view, a man and his dog who had suffered what he'd suffered ought to be awarded much more than any female.

He hadn't actually yet come across any account of compensation awarded to dogs suffering psychological trauma, but he was determined that should be taken into account. Maybe the RSPCA or Blue Cross, who were very caring about sick animals, could give him some free advice on this point. He didn't see going to the expense of consulting the local vet.

He was, however, pretty certain that he'd be a rich man when his case came to be considered in the courts. And that would make the likes of stuck-up Mrs. Prettiflower sit up and take notice when she read about it in the papers. She'd wish then that she'd let him help her make out a claim for the damage to that dead husband of hers. She'd be sorry she'd practically slammed the door in his face.

Arthur found this thought quite comforting as he chopped some chunks of cheese into Scruff's feeding bowl. He selected an almost clean glass from among the pile of unwashed crockery in the kitchen sink and on the draining board. He gave the glass a quick rinse under the tap, then filled it with the remains of the whisky, which he thought must have somehow evaporated. It seemed to have disappeared remarkably quickly. Had he poured some of it on that plant he'd taken to that Mrs. Prettiflower to try and liven it up a bit? He couldn't remember. What a waste if he had.

Grabbing up his supply of pills and his plastic folder of notes, he proceeded into the dining room where, having pushed all the clutter of old unread newspapers, magazines and unopened post on the table to one side, he had every intention to begin in earnest his carefully prepared claim against Smethers & Lybrand.

Taking a swig of whisky to wash down his pills, he pondered how he should begin. "Dear Messrs Smethers and Lybrand…"? No. That wouldn't do. From what those police officers had said both Smethers and Lybrand were dead. So it was no good addressing his claim to them.

"Dear Sirs…"? No. That wouldn't do either.

"To whom it may concern…" Yes. That was better. Good start that. Looked official.

He'd get straight to the point in the next sentence. Tell them how much trouble they had caused him one way and another.

"…After all I have suffered because of your actions, I am now going to…"

Oh no! The bloody biro wasn't working again. He threw it to one side and stamped off in search of a replacement. There *must* be another pen that worked *somewhere* in the house.

It wasn't easy finding things in the Blenkinsop household now that there was so much mess and muddle everywhere. So it took Arthur quite a while to locate another biro under a pile of dirty shirts and underpants on the floor up in the bathroom, by which time he was really feeling most peculiar. When at last he returned with some difficulty to the dining room, he was uncomfortably aware that the table was acting up as if it was on a stormy north sea.

"Whoa there! Shteady she goesh!" he mumbled, grabbing at the edges of the table, sending it crashing against the door, before slumping face down, across the table, knocking the almost empty whisky glass over as he did so. Soon he was dead to the world, fast asleep and snoring noisily.

Scruff, having squeezed through the narrow gap between the partially closed door and the dining table, tried unsuccessfully, to rouse Arthur by reaching up on hind legs to lick his master's flushed face. Scruff had tried to alert Arthur to the fact that he had just thrown up in the kitchen all over the floor and that he now needed to be taken out urgently for a doggy pee. That cheese had not agreed with him. But, there was no response at all from Arthur.

There was still no response from Arthur or from Scruff either, when a key was turned in the front door lock. And, straight through the hall and into the chaotic smelly kitchen, walked Ethel, resplendent in a brand new outfit of red and black, and chic high-heeled, knee-length black leather boots.

27

Ethel took one look around her and was horrified by what she saw.

"Men!" she exclaimed, surveying the neglected state of her kitchen, "Can't leave them alone for five minutes to look after themselves."

The fond thought fleetingly crossed her mind that her Mr. Hardy at Smethers & Lybrand would also probably be feeling just as lost as Arthur without her. She wondered how her lovely Mr. Hardy was managing without her. Then she reminded herself somewhat ruefully that she must put that thought firmly behind her. He wouldn't be her responsibility any more because she wouldn't be returning to work there again – not now.

It was actually rather more than five minutes since she'd walked out on Arthur, she thought guiltily. She and Arthur had both said some terrible things to one another in the heat of the moment when they'd had that flaming row. Things that were best forgotten and should be forgiven.

Ethel had prayed long and hard and asked the Lord to forgive Arthur for hitting her. She, herself, had just about forgiven him, now the bruises had healed well enough for her not to have to wear dark glasses any more. She hoped Arthur was well and truly sorry for his sins, especially after what he'd done to her and she hoped that he'd had time to find out how much he missed her.

As she looked around her, she concluded there was no doubt

whatsoever that she most certainly had been missed. From her examination of the contents, or rather lack of them, in the fridge and kitchen store cupboard, she could see Arthur hadn't been feeding himself properly. She noted with some disapproval the empty whisky and liqueur brandy bottles, fleetingly wondering what kind of emergency had prompted their entire consumption.

What a mess and what an awful smell. Ah well, as soon as she'd changed out of her smart new clothes into the overall she'd left hanging behind the kitchen door the day she left so hurriedly, she would start cleaning things up right away, especially that dog mess all over the kitchen floor. Whatever had Arthur been giving that poor dog to eat?

She fished out a pair of Marigold gloves and the bottle of disinfectant from under the sink and set to work in earnest. Ethel derived great satisfaction from household chores. She had always held the firm belief that cleanliness was next to Godliness and that it was the devil who found work for idle hands. She herself had never been idle, not like Arthur. *And*, he got so much worse since he'd left Bowyers Pharmaceuticals. Mooning and moping around the place like a lost soul! He'd have to pull himself together now, she decided. She'd see to that. There were certain things she had to say to him. But that would have to wait until later.

Upstairs even greater disorder awaited her. Piles of dirty clothes strewn all over the floor, in the bathroom and in the bedroom. And when she looked inside the wardrobe, she was amazed to see almost all her clothes had disappeared. What could have happened to them? Could there have been a break-in during her absence which meant that Arthur wasn't entirely to blame for all the mess after all? But why would a burglar have taken her clothes and not Arthur's? She couldn't think of any reasonable explanation. He or she, if it had been a female burglar, might just as well have taken the lot whilst they were about it, especially that old suit of Arthur's which smelt of moth-balls. That was well past its wearable date. Ah well, it didn't really matter now because she and Arthur weren't going to need any of that old clobber any more. Not according to what she had in mind for their future. She couldn't wait to tell him.

Where was he, by the way? The lazy layabout. He wasn't in the bedroom, lying in bed, glooming over world wide disasters and the goings-on of corrupt politicians reported in the tabloid newspapers. He was probably still stuck in the toilet trying to do the crossword. No. He wasn't there. Ah well, she told herself, wherever he was now lazing about somewhere, he wouldn't be able to do any of that for much longer, No more lying on his backside in bed, staring up at the ceiling, she'd make sure of that. He never could make good use of his time – not like her. All that was going to change after he'd heard what she had to say to him.

"Arthur! Arthur? Are you there?" she called.

No answer. Then, "Scruff? Where are you, boy?"

She called again, shriller and louder.

Still no answer. Ah well, it was a good thing they were both out of the way whilst she got on with giving the place a thorough spring-clean. She'd soon have everything in order again in no time.

She concluded that Arthur must have taken Scruff for a walk. Little did she know that neither of them was in a fit enough state to respond. She shrugged and went on with her cleaning.

★★★

Ethel was not aware of Scruff barking and whining, through the noise of the vacuum cleaner and of her own singing of *Onward Christian Soldiers*. It was only much later when having thoroughly cleaned and polished everything upstairs, she was then about to inspect the state of the dining room. It was with some difficulty she managed to push open the door into the dining room. There she found the dishevelled Scruff and the apparently unconscious Arthur.

Dropping her furniture polish spray and duster, she edged round the gap between table and door and reached out in an effort to rouse him.

"Arthur? Can you hear me, Arthur? It's Ethel."

There was no reaction. She sniffed suspiciously. He'd been *drinking*! That's why there were those empty bottles in the kitchen.

She might have guessed he'd get up to something stupid the moment her back was turned.

He certainly wouldn't have been doing that if she'd been around. He must be drunk – dead drunk. She couldn't abide any form of alcohol, which is why she had signed the pledge as a young girl. In her opinion, strong drink should only ever be taken in a serious medical emergency. She'd seen enough as a child of what drink could do to a family when her father came reeling and roaring home from the Works, having spent most of his weekly earnings in the local pub on a Friday night and then beat up her and her mam. He always said he was sorry and bought them a pea and pie supper as a treat the next day when he was sober. And her soft-hearted mam had invariably forgiven him. But as far as Ethel was concerned, it had hardened her resolve never to touch a drop of alcohol in her life. So finding Arthur like this brought back painful memories.

"Oh Arthur…!" she began.

Just look at the state he was in! She should never have left him on his own, she told herself. He was useless without her around. He wouldn't have ended up in this state if she'd been here.

It was then that she spotted the nearly empty pill container, lying on the table. The stupid fool! What did he think he was doing? Didn't he know those pills should never be taken with alcohol unless...

"Oh My God!" She was glancing at what he had been writing:

"To whom it may concern. After all I have suffered because of your actions, I am going to..."

It was a suicide note! Oh dear Lord, no! What could possibly have caused him to take this terrible action? To destroy the precious gift of life was a mortal sin. It was all her fault for having left him on his own. She should never have done that. May the Lord forgive her.

★★★

The ambulance arrived very promptly after Ethel had rung 999. She, herself, had changed out of her working overall into her smart new outfit again, all ready to accompany Arthur to hospital.

The para-medics were preoccupied with transferring the inert form of Arthur by stretcher into the ambulance when Ruby Kersley appeared on the scene. She was, she had confided earlier to her cousin Mabel, taking her life in her hands in returning to Priory Terrace where *that dreadful man*, the one who'd done away with his wife, lived. But, it was essential that she did so in order to collect some vital items of clean underwear. In this cold northern climate, winter woollies did not dry well out on the clothes line at that time of the year. And she did not want to catch her death of cold, nor did she want be caught out in dirty underwear, if she happened to meet with an unfortunate accident in the street and be taken to hospital, It was a message which had been dinned into her ever since girlhood.

"So you've found the body then?" She called to the paramedics, who having carefully stowed the unconscious Arthur safely inside the ambulance were just emerging from the rear doors of the vehicle. Being somewhat short-sighted, Ruby had failed to notice Ethel in the background, locking her front door behind her.

"About time too," Ruby went on severely. "That poor dear must be in a dreadful state by now."

Oh that poor dear woman! What a way to go! All the same, Ruby couldn't help feeling a glow of satisfaction at having played some small part in bringing to light this gruesome discovery. She was thinking to herself that maybe she'd get a mention in the local papers, or even on TV.

She was suddenly aware that the ambulance men were regarding her with broad grins on their faces. Well, really! A situation such as this one was hardly a matter for laughter! But then, she supposed they were used to all manner of grisly sights in their sort of work and were quite hardened by having to deal with bodies in the kind of state this one must have been in by now.

"That's right, petal. Completely plastered, I'd say," agreed the first para-medic with a cheery wink.

So, that's what he'd done with Ethel, that poor dear woman! Put her body in some wall cavity and plastered it over, just like that Rillington Place murderer who'd disposed of any number of women that way. Ruby had read all about that years ago. She, knew it! She'd suspected it all along. *She* could have been his next victim. Ruby felt herself going all weak at the knees. She leant against the privet hedge for support.

"You all right, Mrs. K?" the question, put to her by a very concerned Ethel, reached Ruby's ears through a kind of haze.

Had she really heard aright? *Ethel?* It *was* Ethel's voice she'd heard speaking to her, wasn't it? Bu—t...but...then—who, what...?

Ruby, unable to answer for the moment, nodded weakly. She turned and stared in amazement. It was Ethel all right. There she was, alive and well, all dressed up to the nines too, standing right in front of her. So, she wasn't...after all, was she? No, of course she wasn't.

Then whose body had just been put in that ambulance? Who was it then that that man had done in? Had he lured some strange woman into the house and done away with her? And where was he now? Out looking for another victim? And, what was she going to tell her cousin Mabel? Still dazed, but pulling herself together with a tremendous effort, Ruby murmured,

"Yes...I'm all right...but I thought you were..."

"In Australia, with my daughter? No! Didn't Arthur tell you? I had family business elsewhere... . Look, I'm sorry, Mrs. K, I have to go with the ambulance now. And you'd better go indoors out of this cold. You're looking quite peaky. Make yourself a nice hot cup of tea. You look as if you could do with one."

Ethel watched Ruby Kershaw totter off back to number 9. The poor old biddy! She really was bad on her feet these days. She ought to get that hip of hers seen to, even if it meant going private.

28

As Ethel settled herself as comfortably as she could beside Arthur in the ambulance, she thought she detected a slight flickering of his eyelids.

"Arthur? It's me. Ethel."

His eyes remained closed but his lips moved slightly in the faintest of whispers. Although Ethel bent low to hear what he was trying to say, none of it made any sense to her:

"Gone. Never coming back…I told them…they said it was murder…trying to murder *me* they were…that cheese…hit him instead…wife's a bloody bitch…Hate her.. Hate all of 'em…"

"Oh Arthur! That's no way to talk," Ethel cut in briskly, "Listen, I've something important to tell you…"

But Arthur was in no fit state to be told anything. He had drifted off into a state of semi-consciousness again. Her news would have to wait.

It would indeed, from what the doctor in charge of the special unit said to Ethel later.

"I'm afraid your husband won't be allowed to come home for some time, Mrs. Blenkinsop. We're transferring him to the psychiatric unit. Not only because of the attempted suicide, which he persistently denies, but also because of his state of mind. He appears to be delusional – all this talk about being murdered by a cheese. Have *you* any idea what could have caused this?"

Ethel had to admit that she could think of nothing, other than that she thought it must have been something to do with the cheese which had made their dog, Scruff, throw up all over the kitchen floor.

She said nothing about how she had abandoned Arthur or of the dreadful row which had preceded it. Apart from her sense of guilt over this, she resented being asked about their private life. Asking her embarrassing questions about their sex life! That was strictly between her and Arthur. It was none of these nosy doctors' business! She wasn't having any of that! Her lips were tightly sealed on that subject. Nor did she tell anyone, least of all Arthur, who probably wouldn't have taken it in anyway – not yet, why she had rushed off to Huddersfield.

"At least I was able to get there in good time," she congratulated herself smugly, "and it must have been a great comfort to her at the end."

Although, in all honesty, her Great Aunt Hetty Agnes Gertrude was not sufficiently *compos mentis* to remember exactly who she was, when Ethel stood patiently at her bedside, waiting for her to breathe her last.

It was very clear from her great aunt's will that the canny old lady had amassed a considerable fortune as a result of her frugal ways and that she'd left it all to Ethel. To begin with, she had never burdening herself with a husband, who would have frittered money away on beer and tobacco. And she'd never indulged in unnecessary luxuries like for instance, soft toilet paper – the sort those puppy dogs used on the telly. Great Aunt Hetty Agnes Gertrude had used carefully cut squares of newspaper in the lavvy all her life. She always said it was the best use for this bumph from her brief reading of it. Fortunately, newspapers had become thicker and thicker over recent years, what with all the supplements they included, especially at the weekends, which more than adequately met her modest needs. In fact, Great Aunt Hetty Agnes Gertrude maintained, it had saved her a fortune.

It was only right, thought Ethel that the money her great aunt had left her should be put to the best possible purpose. One which she, Great Aunt Hetty Agnes Gertrude, would most certainly have approved of. Ethel decided what better use than to spend the money on travelling out to Australia to share this good fortune with her great aunt's namesake, Sharon Hetty Agnes Gertrude and the baby that Sharon was expecting. Of course, when it arrived, the baby would have to be called after her generous benefactress. On the other hand, if it was a boy, which Ethel hoped it wouldn't be because Great Aunt Hetty Agnes Gertrude had never liked boys…well, the kid's father, or even Arthur perhaps, could suggest something suitable Ethel supposed. When he came to his senses again, that it.

He appeared to be sleeping like a baby now as she sat beside the well-sedated Arthur, tucked up like a chipolata sausage in a pastry-encased sausage roll, in his hospital bed. All that was visible of his face was the tip of his red nose and flushed forehead, against the snowy whiteness of the sheets. When she whispered, "Arthur, are you awake?" there was no response. He must be asleep. Gently she took his limp hand in hers. How pathetic he looked. So forlorn and abandoned. And badly in need of a hair-cut, into the bargain. She'd have to see about that, when she got him back home again, that is.

Ethel felt really guilty for having left him as she had done all on his own. After all, he hadn't been all that bad as a husband, not like her own father. Arthur had always let her take charge of all the household affairs and never stood in her way in making decisions over the upbringing of her darling Sharon. And, he'd not been over-demanding in 'the bedroom department' either, especially after they were married. Not like some men, from what she'd overheard from other women, during her temping time with the Busy Bees Secretarial Agency. Well, with God being everywhere, she, herself, after the ill-timed arrival of her darling Sharon that is, had always thought to do 'that kind of thing' with Him looking on, wouldn't have been quite nice, now would it. True Arthur had never embraced the teachings of the Lord, as she had done, in spite of her constant entreaties but maybe she could still bring about changes to his way of thinking when he was under her care again. Looking at him now, he was indeed a lost soul in need of salvation.

Arthur obviously couldn't cope without her. All that mess everywhere in the house! And all those meaningless bits of scribble all over the dining room table. Amongst the pile of unopened post was the letter she had sent him from Huddersfield, telling him that she had prayed to the Lord to forgive Arthur and urging him to pray for forgiveness too. She had added a P.S. in which she reminded him that in accordance with her marriage vows and in spite of everything, she was still prepared to love him 'until Death do us part'. That letter, too was unopened and unread. No wonder he was in such a state. No wonder he had been driven to such extremes. And it was all her fault thought Ethel.

It had taken her ages to clear all that clutter of paper scribblings out of the dining room into the rubbish-bin, and to make the house fresh and clean again. Although, they wouldn't be staying there much longer. Not now. Her mind was firmly made up about that.

Ethel had already decided upon certain plans for their future. She had already made some preliminary enquiries at Hobbit & Moore, the main estate agents in the high street, about putting the house on the market. She hadn't yet mentioned it to Arthur, of course. He was not ready for that kind of information, even though he was no longer rambling on quite so much about brazen widows and lawyers and being murdered by a giant cheese. Poor Arthur! What a state he must have got himself in when she wasn't there to look after him. He must have thought she'd walked out on him for good. The daft lummock. Well, she'd make sure he put all that behind him now that she was back.

A new start in life was just what Arthur needed, Ethel concluded. And, dear Lord, he certainly needed her. That was painfully obvious. A new start in a new country. A new start for both of them. Together. For better or for worse.

29

Eeeeh!" The pitch of that shriek emitted by Bruce Mackoy's bride-to-be, Sharon, upon reading her mother's airmail letter, would have shattered a wine glass had there been one in the immediate vicinity in their New South Wales suburban home. It reached Bruce's ears even though his head was stuck inside the bonnet of Sheila, his beloved limo.

Sheila was the great love of his life and had been so ever since he'd acquired her. She had been pretty clapped out when he first brought her back to the workshop adjoining the shed, which housed the two other cars which constituted his taxi and car hire business. *'Bruce Mackoy'll getya anywhere anytime'* was his proud boast. He'd worked on her night and day to restore her to the gleaming beauty that she now was. She was a joy to behold, every single part of her, right down to her last nut and bolt, all of which were loving checked regularly by Bruce. And after all that effort, she was much too precious to take out on the road. She wasn't that kind of a car. Although, as an act of supreme unselfishness, he supposed he just might take her out of the garage on his wedding day, whenever that might be.

Reluctantly Bruce withdrew his attention from contemplating the intricacies of Sheila's moving parts, in order to respond appropriately to the call of the second love of his life.

"Wassup Shar?" he bellowed, in a voice that echoed round the neighbourhood. "It's not the ba'y is it, pumpkin?"

Strewth! He still couldn't believe he was going to be a dad so soon. *"B. Mackoy AND Junior'll getya anywhere, anytime!"* would be the new slogan for his business operations henceforth. That was going to look real beaut right over the garage workshop!

Sharon sighed. She wished he wouldn't call her 'Shar' or yell details of their private life out like that for all the neighbours to hear. It was so common. Whatever was her mother going to think when she met him!

So far, Ethel had only seen photos of Bruce. She had said somewhat cautiously that she thought he looked like a 'very nice young man'. Knowing full well that whatever she said about her daughter's choice of new partner, Sharon would make her own mind up anyway. Indeed, Bruce did look good in photos, particularly in that one on the internet when he and Sharon had first met via 'Date-a-Mate'.

It was more or less on the strength of that first photo that Sharon booked herself on a flight to Australia at the earliest opportunity, having made up her mind to mate this newfound date asp. He looked much too good a catch to be allowed to slip through the net.

She'd certainly been smitten by the appearance of this hunky guy who was quite unlike her ex, a minor public school boy she'd met in a posh night-club. She'd been swept off her feet by him. Although, his insufferable snob of a mother had made it all too plain right from the start that she had never really taken to Sharon. So that marriage had been doomed from the start. Especially as he, the ex, had turned out to have an incurable nanny complex. Sharon considered she was well rid of *him*.

Bruce, when he and Sharon met for the first time at Sydney airport. was mighty pleased with his side of the internet 'Date-a-Mate' bargain. Constantly goaded by his five older brothers, he had decided it was high time for him fill a gap in his love life, possibly on a permanent basis.

Sharon decided that things had worked out well with Bruce so far, even though she had been somewhat surprised at the suburban surroundings she found herself in now. This wasn't quite what she'd had pictured from having watched all those episodes of *Neighbours* on the T.V. And another thing she discovered to her disappointment, Bruce's transport business was by no means as large as she had imagined it would be. It certainly wasn't on the scale of National Express or Stagecoach, back home. Still, in time she and he would work on that together, after the arrival of the baby, of course.

The unexpected speed at which she had become pregnant had taken them both by surprise. She could feel the baby kicking within her now as, still clutching her mother's letter, she waddled heavily across the yard. She could hardly wait to share the good news to Bruce.

"They're coming. They'll be here any minute. I've just had this letter Oh Brucie! It's all so exciting, isn't it…?"

He dropped his spanner in amazement. Although quick in his responses in some parts of his anatomy, Bruce was rather slow when it came to cerebral activities.

'*They?*' That's what she'd said, wasn't it. Geez! Not just one then but *two* of them. That'd be twins, or even more maybe! That letter Shar said she'd just received must be from the gyno at the hospital, where she was, he supposed, receiving regular check-ups just like his Sheila was being given in the garage work-shop. Just wait till he told this piece of news to those five older brothers of his and other rellies back home! That would certainly show 'em!

"Aw pumpkin. That's real ace!"

Sharon eyed him with some surprise, mingled with delight at his enthusiasm. She wasn't altogether sure what his reaction would be to the news that her parents would soon be joining them in Aussieland.

"Yes! And it's not just for a visit either. They'll be staying here with us for good."

He was staring at her in complete bewilderment. It hadn't occurred to him that they wouldn't be keeping them once they arrived! Even if there was going to be more than one of them. Where was Shar thinking of sending them then? He'd be dead against having any of them adopted. How could he put this to her in her present state? As he pondered over this delicate question, Sharon seized the opportunity to continue.

"Of course, we'll need a much bigger house."

Well, yes, he realised that. Their present accommodation was a bit cramped, even now, for just the two of them.

"And they'll be a great help to you in your business."

'They'. She'd said it again! So it must be true. Although, he thought she was jumping the gun a bit by saying they'd be a help in the business. That would be some time ahead. Besides, they didn't even know what sex they were going to be yet.

"They'll soon pick things up," Sharon went on, "especially my mum. And Dad'll be a great help too when he's well again. He's good at figures."

"Mum? Dad?" Bruce digested this further information slowly and in stunned silence. In fact, it took a little while, as Sharon read out the details of Ethel's letter with the news of her sudden windfall, for this startling new development to dawn upon Bruce. Especially as it involved a readjustment of expectations in relation to the addition to his family.

In the short space of time they had been together, Bruce had come to realise that his Shar was the kind of gal who always got what she wanted. He knew she was missing her mum. She had mentioned it several times. And, although she hadn't said much about her Dad, Bruce assumed she must be missing him too. So, if that's what was going to keep her happy for her pommy oldies to join them, then why not? She said they were arranging to bring their dog out with them as well. Bruce liked dogs. They'd be one big happy family – her dad, Arthur, her mum, Ethel *and* a dog. Geez! It was all going to be just ace!

30

When Justin Walker told me what I'd done, I was thrown into a state of complete confusion. He must have thought I was some kind of shameless merry widow on the prowl when my messages came up on his screen. I explained to him as discreetly as possible how, at Cathy's suggestion, because she was so much better informed on the subject than I was, that I'd been researching the strictly fictional aspects of sex for my next book. Although, I had to confess that I wasn't so sure now that this was such good idea. I've really gone right off the idea, after what's been happening here.

Justin nodded sympathetically and I noticed the sparkle of interest in his eye when Cathy's name was mentioned. Fortunately, he, being the perfect gentleman he is, was most tactful about what I had done. Even so, I was so embarrassed! I've no idea how this could have happened. And I thought I was making such good progress in using my new computer.

I don't think I'll be sending any more emails ever again. I even contemplated trying to somehow retrieve my old typewriter by putting an advertisement under 'Wanted' in the local paper, appealing to the boy scout's dad who'd bought it at the jumble sale to sell it back to me, or maybe exchange this accursed new-fangled machine for it.

However, Justin persuaded me not to do anything so rash, by assuring me he would not give up teaching me until I was completely computer-literate. He was certain, or so he said, I would come to regard this one-eyed monster more favourably when I realised what possibilities it presented for me.

"It'll open up a whole new world for you," he assured me.

"How wonderful," I said, trying my best to sound more enthusiastic than I actually felt.

It appears that all those messages which I'd been sending on my progress in exploring sex in modern literature, as I thought for Cathy's eyes only, had somehow been circulated to everyone in my email address book. This included Justin and several of Marcus's ex-colleagues and, of course, Liz Marley as well. Although, that would be all right because Liz would be bound to realise that it was all to do with research for the new book I'd mentioned to her. But this just goes to show how people can be given entirely the wrong ideas by accidentally touching the wrong button.

So, in spite of Justin's promises, from now on my communications will be carried out strictly by letter-writing or telephoning only.

As a matter of fact, I was on the point of writing to Liz Marley again, since she hadn't been responding at all to any of my communications for quite some time. I thought that perhaps she needed to be reassured about my intention to get started on some really serious new work in the near future. However, a letter arrived in the post that morning from Liz's PA:

'Dear Margot,' it said, 'This is to let you know that I shall be dealing with yourself and Liz's other authors, until Liz returns from extended sick leave. In the meantime, do send me your proposed manuscript on *Pinkie the Elephant's Renaissance* which I look forward to reading, Best regards, Fiona.'

Oh dear! It looks as if confusion can arise in every form of communication. No doubt Fiona, poor girl, is overwhelmed with everything she has to deal with in Liz's absence so perhaps she hadn't had time to go through my file properly.

'*Pinkie the Elephant's Renaissance*' – what an idea, I ask you! Although, on the other hand…maybe '*Pinkie*' is due for a revival. In any case, all that business over the emails has quite put me off the whole idea of sex and the older reader. I'll have to give it some more serious thought. Or perhaps some other kind of book entirely. After all, there were all those carefully compiled notes made by dear Marcus about the history of cheese-making, tracing it right back to Roman times. It would be a pity if all that research were wasted. Or, maybe I should be writing the book that Marcus had always refused to consider. Memories of his childhood in a place that no longer officially exists. And then *his* 'renaissance', symbolising as it does, the experience of others like him who, having survived against overwhelming odds, have with great courage progressed onwards and upwards.

Anyway, there's no time to dwell on such matters now. I'll think about it later, during my stay in Majorca.

I've far too much to do now. There are several vital items, like sun protection cream and swim suits, still to be bought for a holiday where the sun is likely to be shining more strongly and the water more inviting for swimmers, than in this northerly region. And, I must remember to buy a 'Get Well' card to send off from Majorca to Liz Marley. It sounds very much as if she herself, poor lass, could do with a holiday in the sun somewhere.

It was whilst I was undertaking these chores that I bumped into Sandra…something or other…again. Her second name escapes me, but she was at Marcus's funeral. There were too many people there at that sad time for me to recall them all. However, I recognised her immediately, not just because of her striking red hair. It was also because of her dazzling smile and because she had been so kind and solicitous in expressing her condolences, that I remembered her more clearly than some of the others. She was glowing with some kind of inner radiance now. I noticed that her shopping basket was loaded with jars of olives and numerous packets of all kinds of cheese. I assumed she must be preparing for some kind of a cheese and wine party. But it wasn't so.

She was smiling at me now with that dazzling smile of hers.

"I always get these weird cravings for olives and cheese when I'm pregnant," she informed me, somewhat apologetically.

"Marcus, my husband, loved cheese," I replied rather foolishly, which appeared to embarrass and distress her. I was trying desperately to bring to mind something more appropriate to say, when she blurted out,

"Charles wasn't to blame, it wasn't his fault. It *was* an accident, you know."

"Charles?"

"Yes, my husband, Charles. You do understand, don't you?"

She was looking at me so anxiously, I felt I had to reassure her that she had my approval. God only knows why she thought it necessary for me to know such intimate details of her baby's conception. Perhaps this was some kind of *Ancient Mariner* syndrome some women experienced during pregnancy.

"Y-e-s," I replied uncertainly, reaching out to pat her arm reassuringly, "But you are pleased about the baby, aren't you?"

"Oh yes, of course, we are. We're delighted. Both of us. And the girls too. Our daughters, that is. Although Nicola was rather hoping for a pony, she really is thrilled at the thought of a new baby."

I, somewhat self-consciously, joined in her laughter. She radiated such happiness. Lucky infant being born into a family where he, or she would be the centre of so much love, I thought.

"They are so looking forward to having a baby brother," she added for good measure.

I wondered how she could be so certain of the baby's sex,

at this stage. She sounded very positive about it. I suppose with modern technology such things are no longer the well-kept wonderful nine-month long secret they once were.

"Congratulations!" I said, trying desperately to think of some further comment but nothing came to mind.

"Thanks!" She gave me another of her dazzling smiles. "Good to see you again. And you're looking so well, too. You're coping OK?"

She didn't appear to expect an answer as she hurriedly added, "I must dash. Take good care of yourself. Bye now."

Coda

Cruising gently down the motorway in Justin's car, to meet Cathy at the airport, I was still puzzling over those odd remarks made by that Sandra something-or-other about the 'accident'.

I couldn't help wondering just how many of us come into this world as the result of 'an accident'. And, then how many of us leave this world because of... . No! I would not allow myself to pursue that thought any further. And yet, I also couldn't help thinking, why are any of us here on this Earth at all? Are we all just the result of some cosmic accident within the Universe, as some scientists would have us believe? Or, are we no more than the mere quiver of wings of mayflies, passing briefly through into Eternity ? Or, perhaps we are, each one of us, like notes of music – small but significant parts of some grand divine orchestral composition? God alone knows. The answer is beyond the grasp of our human understanding.

It was a grey day with sullen clouds overhead and rain, like giant tears, streaming endlessly down the windscreen. It would be good to get away to somewhere where I hoped we would find sunshine and clear blue skies.

We travelled on in silence, each with our own thoughts to the accompaniment of a Chopin tape playing softly in the background. To Justin's way of thinking, I supposed this was a suitable prelude to our forthcoming visit to Majorca. We'd be staying not far from Valldemossa, that romantic place where, as legend would have it, Chopin and George Sand had lived and loved together.

"It's all much too complicated," I said to myself, thinking back yet again to my recent encounter with Sandra something-or-other. I must have voiced this thought aloud, or else Justin's sensitive antennae had picked up the message. He glanced at me with kindly concern and said awkwardly,

"You're bound to feel you're missing Marcus right now. Dashed bad luck that he went so suddenly, the way he did. But it happened and he'd have wanted you to move on, you know. We all have to move on, one way or another."

"Yes. I know. You're right. Cathy said something of that sort. She said: onwards and upwards."

Justin smiled and nodded without comment. I could see at a glance that Cathy had certainly won his approval and that this last remark of mine had set him off on some deeply personal train of thought in which I played no major part.

"Margot's not really my type," he was thinking. Although, he had wondered fleetingly if she had developed a crush on him when he received that clutch of strange emails. Dashed embarrassing that would have been! But, thank God, she had managed to convince him that it was all a mistake. Anyway, she was much too housewifey for his taste. Although, in early widowhood she had fleetingly awakened his protective instincts, it was not the same kind of feeling the delectable Cathy had aroused in him when he first clapped eyes on her at dear old Marcus's send-off.

Decent chap, old Marcus, all things considered. Not being one of the old public school brigade. Steady and reliable. Probably somewhat unadventurous with regard to women, he'd imagine, since Marcus had remained married for all those years to the same woman. How boringly conservative was that in this day and age! Anyway, one shouldn't think ill of the dead. And, had it not been for Marcus popping his clogs so unexpectedly, he'd never have had the opportunity to meet Cathy and invite her and Margot to his villa in Majorca.

Now, she, Cathy, was certainly his kind of woman! Cultured, soignée, sophisticated and blonde. She didn't look the marrying kind, thank God. He'd been careful to avoid that sort of commitment ever since his last disastrous marriage. It had not put him off women per se, however, especially if they were the well-upholstered Marilyn Monroe kind of blondes. Though of course, Cathy was more of a matchstick catwalk model than some of his previous amours, nevertheless she was most strikingly blonde. At least for the time being, although women did have a capricious way of changing their hair colour from time to time. Bless their adorable little hearts!

Unpredictable, irresistible, fascinating creatures – women. He'd loved – and left many of them in his time, even more so since his third wife, Constance, had walked out on him after a remarkably short spell of conjugal bliss. In actual fact, it had been a rather stormy relationship right from the start. He'd never been able to understand her outbursts of jealousy over his occasional brief affairs. Or to fathom out why she had finally deserted him in floods of angry tears. Why hadn't she believed him when he brought her peace offerings of flowers, chocolates and the sort of little trinkets most women love, to assure her that she was the one he loved most in all the world, the jewel in his crown? She, on her part, had never really understood him and his need to love and to be loved by more than one woman.

Parting from Constance had not exactly been 'such sweet sorrow'. His pain had been intensified by learning later from a mutual acquaintance that Constance had blossomed in a new-found loving relationship, having sought consolation in the arms of someone called Charlie. And then the greatest blow of all to his manhood had been when he learned that 'Charlie' was in fact short for 'Charlotta'. To have been jilted by Constance for another woman was the final straw. It had left him feeling bitter for a while and consequently he had hardened his heart with the resolve never to let himself be hurt again.

However, in the years that followed the break-up of that particular marriage, he had many reasons to be thankful that during the early days of his infatuation with Constance he had purchased the Valldemossa property as a love nest and, that as part of the divorce settlement, he had succeeded in hanging on to it. It was a place of romantic possibilities, which had never failed to meet his expectations over subsequent years. And, he reminded himself, in just a few hours he'd be there yet again – this time with delectable Cathy.

His face lit up at the prospect of anticipated pleasures that awaited him. He hoped Margot would be able to find something or other to occupy herself during their stay since he did not fancy a ménage à trois. Ah yes, of course, she'd probably be glad to have some quiet time on her own to get on with that sexy book she'd vaguely mentioned she was thinking of writing when she was doing all that research on the computer. So there was no need to worry about her. She'd be well occupied. All taken care of in fact.

I was glad I had remembered to pack plenty of biros and A4 notebooks with which to busy myself during our stay in Majorca. It was something of a relief to know that when we finally arrived at our holiday destination, whilst he and Cathy were becoming better acquainted, I would be able to set to work without any distractions on drafting – what was it to be? Would it *Pinkie the Elephant's* new adventures, some non-fiction work about cheese, or would it be Marcus's story? I had yet to decide.

I became aware that Justin was smiling kindly as he glanced across again at me. Such a considerate man. The kind of man you feel really safe with. I was very touched by his thoughtful concern.

"I'm so sorry," I said, "my thought were miles away. Did you say something?"

"Onwards and upwards," he murmured. "That's the spirit! No point in looking back. Even God can't change the past." Then he added, "Dammit, if it's the music that's making you sad, choose something else."

He reached across and opened up the glove compartment for me to select some other tape. He certainly had a fine collection there to suit all tastes, neatly stacked beside a bottle of very chic and expensive after-shave. From the pile of tapes, I chose one of Marcus's favourite pieces and then settled back to the wonderful strains of the last movement of Beethoven's *Choral Symphony*. It was an expression of sheer joy and hope for the future.

END